WOMAN IN BLACK

WOMAN IN BLACK

Never give up!

John Darling

John Darling

To order additional copies of this book, contact:
Xlibris Corporation
1-888-795-4274
www.Xlibris.com
Orders@Xlibris.com
28826

CONTENTS

Love

Heroism

Adventure

One Small Play About God

LOVE

I KNOW WHY

Inspiration

Higgins liked his new job, even if it only turned out to be a temporary assignment as his agency explained to him it might be. The pay was good, the company was reputable, and any time spent here would look good on his resume. He also enjoyed the work he was asked to carry out.

His mind was churning over a new project when he first heard the scratching noise behind him. Turning to see what was causing the sound, he observed a stunning woman dressed in a floral, almost Hawaiian style, floor length dress. The dress showed off every curve of her lovely, statuesque body.

She was standing at the Daily Stat Sheet making recordings of mail receipts. This meant that she must have been a clerk somewhere—which, as a man, seemed impossible to him given her beauty.

When she realized that Higgins was gaping at her, she turned to him and said, "Hello". Then she flashed the most brilliant smile he had ever seen. It lit up her pale blue eyes and gave them an impish, intelligent, quality; a quality that enhanced her beauty even more.

She then finished her task and turned to leave. Higgins was still gaping at her when she looked back, smile still in place, and said, "I'll see you later."

"If only in my dreams." he thought as he watched her walk away. The rest of his day was spent in a mild stupor as he thought about the brief encounter.

Dialogue

Higgins fidgeted in his chair. It was his last day of work. Across from him sat Talea, his best and most beautiful friend. After two years of lunches, like this, exchanges of ideas, thoughts, and even mild flirting, he realized now that he did not know much about her. Still, he loved her deeply. Now he had to tell her this, after today, there may be no more chances.

He knew she was married and though she rarely spoke of him, she seemed to be happy with her husband. But, Higgins was consumed. She had to know his true feelings even though he expected nothing to come of the revelation.

To sit next to her like this without her knowing was agony; a gnawing, physical pain that he could no longer endure. She had to know if only to relieve him of his distress.

What she would never know is that he was leaving his job because of his feelings for her. He could never lay that burden on her, nor would he ever demand that she love him in return. She never once, in the time he had known her, acted as anything more than a friend, his best friend.

He was not sure when he first realized just how much he loved her. There was no overt act on her part; no extra word of tenderness, no special hairstyle she tried that triggered this feeling. One day it just came to him, he loved her more than he thought it was ever possible to love anyone.

Over the time, since that unknown day, he made his plans to leave. He made up excuses, stating openly his dissatisfaction with his long commute to work, unhappiness with his dead-end job, and a desire to do different, more challenging work, though he meant only a little of this. He even told her that he was going to be more aggressive in his efforts to become a free-lance writer and so he needed more time to do so.

This last part was true, if for Talea only. He had let her read a few of his works while he told no one else that he had this interest. She enjoyed his writing and encouraged him to do more, telling him that he was in the wrong line of work, urging him to either chase his fantasy or live life as an unfulfilled dreamer. She was like that.

"I will miss you Talea." he stated for the fifth time, "If for no other reason than you are one person who can stand to read the drivel that I call short stories."

Before she could object, he went on, "I know you like my narratives and I appreciate your interest in them, which is why I would like you to read something now, if you don't mind? It is the climax of a story I am writing. It is the dialogue of the protagonist who needs to reveal something to a woman he loves but he doesn't know how to tell her. So he pretends to give her something to read for commentary, when he wants her to read it, in reality, for context."

Extending an envelope to her, he said, "Please, Talea, do this one last thing for me. I have been working on this for over two years."

"Of course, Allan. I would love to read it."

Opening the envelope, her lustrous eyes took in the words.

She read, "I know why Paris would kidnap Helen and take her to his kingdom of Troy. I know why Romeo could not stand the pain of living without Juliet. I know why Napoleon would attempt to conquer the world for Josephine.

Since I met you, I discovered the kind of love—obsession—that drives men to achieve more than they could or should on their own. The adage about a woman being behind every good man is true except the woman is actually in front of the man. Men strive for the stars in hopes of catching the eye of the woman they are pursuing.

I have never let my love for you propel me to be as demonstrative as those that I mentioned, but it is no less great or less passionate then theirs. We have always been a perfect pair. I have never felt the need to change or accomplish incredible feats so I could impress you. You always made me feel that I was a worthy man just as I am. This part of you is more of a reason to love you than any other reason I could ever imagine.

You are every where I go; you are in everything I do. Even the smallest actions bring you to my mind.

Last night I was sitting in a bar, alone, but I was not sad or lonely because you were next to me. When the jukebox played a certain love song, I reached out and took your hand. You turned and smiled to me and I began to weep tears of joy just 'knowing' that you were with me. I love you so much.

I can't recall all the occasions when you were with me like that. Even at the silliest times, I think about how things would be if you loved me, as I love you.

I sit at home alone working a crossword puzzle, and I can hear you laugh at how clever I am for knowing what comprised the Iberian Peninsula. I could see your face light up as I point out some small fact that you didn't know. You would drink in this new knowledge, adding it to your superior intellect; a side of you that I think you deny due to your beauty. But then, that is the most endearing part of the being that is you. You are intelligent and kind without being aware of the fact that you possess both of the attributes.

Sleeping has become nearly impossible for me. I can't make it through an entire night anymore. I wake up and wonder what you are dreaming about. I hope against hope that I am the subject. Then I can't get back to sleep, then I cry, then I do go back to sleep for a while, only wanting you to be in my dreams.

I feel as though my life is in total discord right now. My body wants to act one way, but my mind will not allow it. I am being torn in two. I want to hold you and kiss you while confessing my love, but my intellect will not let me. I know that it is not my place to do this and I would never do anything to complicate your life. As long as you are happy, in whatever form that takes, I will be happy. It is important to me that you are happy."

Talea looked up after the last line. Higgins knew why: he had voiced the very same phrase to her countless times.

Her eyes seemed to flicker. Her mouth began to tilt downward. She turned her eyes back to the paper, head bowed. When she looked up the smile had returned to her face, but her eyes showed a hint of sadness.

She read on, "Someday I hope that you will know the depths of my love if for no other reason than to show you that you can be loved like this and that you are worthy of a love like this.

My beautiful friend. I will never forget you, but now I must go to pursue other dreams and leave you free to pursue yours. Just know that no matter what you do, no matter where you go, you will always be with me in my mind."

Talea slowly let the papers fall into her lap.

"Well? What did you think of it?"

She sat silent for a moment, then looked away from him while replying, "Any woman would be honored to be loved so . . ."

Her voice trailed off to a whisper.

She handed the paper back to Higgins. He took out a pen, signed the last page and returned it to her.

"Keep it my lovely friend. Someday, if I become famous, it may be worth something."

With that he stood up and left the building for the last time.

Epilog

Higgins opened his eyes, still glassy from the effect of the mild stroke he suffered and the drugs the doctors were administering. He wondered whom the new nurse was and why she was sitting next to him holding his hand.

Her eyes were pale blue; her face had a youthful, familiar essence about it even though her head was topped with a crown of lustrous gray.

"Talea?"

"Yes, Allan, it is Talea."

"But how . . . ?"

"How did I know you were sick?"

"Yes . . ."

"Allan, the most famous author in our area could not fall ill without the press reporting it. I came as soon as I had heard. How could I not?"

"I love you."

"I know that, Allan. I've known it since the day you let me read the climax of that short story. I was so happy that it was the one that launched your fame, becoming a movie as well as the catalyst for your first best selling book of stories."

"You knew I meant you?"

"Allan, you are a wonderful and gifted writer, but I know you too well. You could not fool me, but then you did not try to fool me did you? You wanted me to know without telling me directly."

"I did."

"Well I knew, Allan. Your plan worked to that end. When I heard about your book, I bought it. When I heard about the movie, I saw it—many times. My husband never understood why I cried in certain scenes that lead no one else to tears."

With the mention of her husband, Higgins wearily turned his head away, trying to force his face into the pillow so he did not have to look at her.

"He passed on, Allan."

He turned back to look at her.

"Just last year. He was a wonderful man, Allan. He loved me and took care of me. But when he died, I did try to find you. You were always such a recluse, though. No one knew, or would tell me, how to contact you. Your agent said you did not even read the fan mail he sent on to you."

"I shut out the world. After I left you, I could not live outwardly in it. There were too many things that would remind me of you; the pains caused by these thoughts were more than I could bear. I am a weak man, Talea."

"To the contrary, Allan. You are the strongest kind of person. You love me, Allan. Seemingly, more than any man could ever love a woman, yet you respected my marriage. You were always a gentleman. Most men would have succumbed to the urge to possess the woman of their dreams and would have pursued her at any price. You held all your desire inside. A struggle so great that I cannot imagine how much it cost you in terms of strength. I wonder if any man has ever known or ever will know."

Tears came to his eyes; they spilled down his cheeks and on to his bed sheets. Talea wiped them up with a small towel. Her touch was as gentle as he remembered. His hand took hers. She smiled that wonderful smile.

"How did you manage to get past my 'guards' to see me, my love? I am sure my agent left strict orders."

"Why Allan, I just showed them my pass." She reached for her handbag sitting on the foot of his bed.

"Pass? What pass, dear?"

She took some pages out of the yellowed envelope she had retrieved from her purse. Handing him the pages, she said, "This one dear. The one you gave me so many years ago."

He looked at the faded words on the paper and on the last page he saw his name scrawled. It was the discourse he gave her the last time he had seen her.

He smiled.

"Couldn't get any money for it I see."

"Man has never produced enough money to buy that from me, dear."

"They are all you, Talea."

"All who, love?" She asked as she returned the manuscript to her handbag. "All the women. In my stories. They are all you. When Maria walked for miles in the snow to be with Julio, you were out there in that bitter cold. When Alaina wrongly went to jail just so James could be free, you were the one who donned the prison garb. When Tereza sat by Enrique's side, nursing him back to health, you were the one who gave him his medicine and tended his wounds. All of them encompassed some part of you. There was never any other woman, ever. Not in fiction or in reality."

She sat back at this revelation. Then bowed her head as her mind mulled it over. He had seen her do this hundreds of times. Finally, she looked up and smiled.

"I love you, Allan."

"And I love you, Talea. How could I not?"

THE END

CRASH AND BURN

K ristie hoped.
     She hoped that the near stranger she invited to an after work get together with her co-workers would not turn out to be an insipid beast like so many of her past men friends.

She had met Brett once, so he claimed, at a party where his friend was playing drums in a reggae band. She remembered the night; she'd had too much to drink and felt awful the next day. Brett told her that it had been rather late and he was on his way home when a mutual friend introduced them. They had only said hello to each other and nothing else. She vaguely remembered the incident but not him—at least not clearly. She had a hazy recollection of a man who was dressed too well for the occasion and who, like all the other men she met, looked her over like she was milk a chocolate candy bar and he was a kid with a dollar.

But that image didn't reconcile with the image in her mind of the man she worked with on so many occasion. Brett was someone she had known for some time, but he was located in another part of her company in another town and though the offices were only a few miles apart, they had never met except on that one occasion.

In the following year after that party, they exchanged hundreds of emails regarding a project they were both working on and had spoken on the phone numerous times. He seemed like a hard working, intelligent, decent man. Just the kind of man she always wanted to meet.

He once paid her a compliment about a picture of her that had appeared in a company magazine, but other than that, he never flirted with her and was ever a gentleman towards her. That frustrated her a little especially since she had heard from other women that he was roughly handsome and quite single. None of the women she new in his facility had ever dated him nor did they know anyone who had.

As other people from her work began to gather, she wondered if she would recognize him if she saw him.

*   *   *

Brett spotted the slim blonde in the tight pink top and bell-bottom blue jeans the minute she walked in. Could that be Kristie? If it was, her picture and his spotty memory of her had not done her justice. She was extremely beautiful.

He was nervous.

Ever since the night of the reggae party a year or so earlier, he had wanted to meet her again. Their fleeting exchange of words and glances had stayed in his mind from that time on.

He wanted to call her the next day and ask her out, but he did not have her home phone number and he never asked women out on company time. Though it was not prohibited for him to do so, he never felt comfortable with it.

He had come to the bar a little early so he could have a drink to calm down a little before he met her again. He wondered if she would recognize him.

As she walked past him, he felt a stab of disappointment. Maybe he should just leave; she was much too pretty for him anyway. While watching her walk by in the reflection of the mirror behind the bar he saw his own face. Not a pretty sight, but he never had much trouble getting dates. He figured, with an inner laugh, that it must have been his charm that attracted women to him.

If nothing else, he was fit. He went to the gym every day, attended Pilates and martial arts training each twice a week, and he ate a good balanced diet—the only kind of diet that really works.

Still, his hands shook as he lifted his drink. Why, he didn't know, it was not like she was a total stranger. Kristie and he had communicated with each other almost daily since they were both working on the same project for their respective areas of their company. She was bright, witty, and seemed very modest. Just the kind of woman he had always wanted to meet.

No, he would stay at the bar for a while and see if he could get up the nerve to approach her.

He ordered another drink and waited for courage to come to him.

*   *   *

It was a warm night in Southern California even though it was mid-September so everyone had voted to sit out in the patio area. Kristie took the seat at the head of the tables her group had moved together. She knew everyone sitting in front of her. A pang of disappointment went through her as she realized that everyone who told her they would join her was here, everyone except for Brett. Had he decided not to come and not told her? That didn't seem like him since, in his work, he was always so dependable.

She listened to and engaged in the small talk around the table. Most of it was about work, which bored her. She wanted desperately to be able to talk about other things, maybe about the arts or sciences, to someone who would listen even if they did not understand. Brett had always seemed to be like that. He was even an author who had stories and articles published in various places. She had read one of his philosophical papers on Selfishness and found it to be very uplifting, but he wasn't here and she was disappointed.

She looked up from listening to the latest bit of gossip gratuitously passed to her by a woman she barely knew, to see a man emerge from the inner darkness of the bar. Could that be Brett?

She hoped so. As he came striding towards her table she summed him up. He was dressed in all black, including shiny black boots. The only coloration on him was a spot on his t-shirt that looked like some sort of fire ring. He wore wrap around sunglasses and his build was, well, very nice. The thin cloth of the t-shirt bulged around his arms and his chest, his waist was slim and tight. There was a slight bulge around his "love handles" but she could live with that. Besides, she liked Brett already without really knowing what he looked like.

He walked over to the group and looked like he was about to say something, but then he closed his mouth as a look of confusion came over his face. No one else seemed to notice him.

*   *   *

Putting down his drink, Brett decided to just go ahead and join the group. If the beautiful woman was Kristie, then he just had to meet her. The worst that could happen would be that it was not her. If it was, he didn't see her turning him away in any situation, much less in front of a bunch of co-workers. She had invited him and they did work for the same company.

Striding to the door, he planned to walk casually over to the table, fully prepared to introduce himself to her.

She was easy to spot on the patio. Her golden hair and her dazzling smile set her off from every other woman out there. He hung back in the darkness of the bar, momentarily, to watch her as she interacted with the group around her. Her blue eyes flashed as she talked with who ever wanted her attention at the moment. Brett was beginning to feel intimidated and unsure of himself again. Maybe another drink?

Then she looked up from the person talking to her, her eyes seemed to cast about the crowd as if she was looking for someone. His heart leapt. Maybe she was looking for him? After a few minutes of this, she looked back upon the crew around the table with a hint of sadness on her face. No one seemed to notice it.

He went out into the fading sunlight to meet her. When he got to the edge of the table, she looked up on him with a radiance in her eyes so powerful, he was struck dumb. Like a fish out of water, he stood awkwardly with his mouth half open, not knowing what to do next.

*   *   *

Kristie knew it was him. She sensed his unease and thought of a way to assuage it.

While looking at the group as if he were not there, she said, "I invited Brett Jameson to this party. Does anyone know who he is or what he looks like?"

No one did. But Brett understood her saving grace and he wanted to kiss her for it.

"I think I know who he is.", he responded, "He is a rather homely guy, who is not too bright either. He works somewhere in Newbury Park, of all places."

The group looked at him in silence. It was obvious no one there knew who he was, so why would this stranger stand up and deprecate a fellow worker of theirs?

He laughed.

"And of course, he would be me," he added with a smile.

This brought a round of uneasy laughter from everyone except Kristie. She was still looking up at him with her dazzling smile while laughing heartily.

He looked around for a vacant bar stool like the kind everyone was sitting on. Finding one, he placed it right next to her, causing the guy who obviously wanted to go home with her, based on his nearness to her, to move aside. The man looked as if he were going to say something, so Brett turned his back on him showing the flaming name and logo of his martial arts school. The man moved over without a word.

Brett chuckled to himself about how easily people were cowed anymore. The man didn't know if he had just bought the shirt or if he had actually been attending the school for the past 5 years, which was the truth.

Kristie noticed the silent interaction and understood what Brett had done.

"So, do you really go to that school, or did you just by the shirt?" she asked as she bent her head close to whisper in his ear.

Her being so close to him was almost more than Brett could handle. He could feel her warmth and smell her soft perfume, which made his knees weak even though he was sitting down, but it was her intuitiveness that impressed him more than anything. She was obviously as insightful as she was intelligent.

"I have been attending classes there for a few years, Kristie. Master Yi finally decided to give me a shirt for all my hard work. It is a great honor and I wear it proudly."

"As you should, Brett. It is difficult to stay with something that physical for so long. So, you must be a Black Belt?"

"I should be, Kristie. But I am a lazy student. I know all that I need to know to be one, but I don't like to test. So I have stopped at Brown Belt, which is the first level of the Upper Belts. I felt that was enough of an accomplishment for me."

Understanding perfectly, Kristie replied, "Different people want different things."

Unable to control himself, he gently took hold of her hand, below the table out of sight of the group, who seemed to not be paying any attention to them anyhow.

She didn't pull back or resist.

"Thank you for inviting me, Kristie. I was surprised when I got the invitation." leaning closer to her, he whispered, "Normally I wouldn't come to something like this, but since you were going to be here . . ."

"I wasn't sure if you would come. I've wanted to meet you—again—for sometime, but I wasn't sure if you felt the same way. You're always so polite and kind to me on the phone, but never forward."

The waitress came over and Brett ordered a "Cosmopolitan" (a concoction of something called triple sec, cranberry juice and vodka Kristie proudly informed him) for her while he joked that he would have a "metropolitan"— just a glass of draft for him.

As she went to get their orders, they put their heads so close together; they were almost cheek to cheek. Brett could feel his inner temperature rising as Kristie's warm breath fell upon his face when she spoke.

They sat that way, just talking, about everything and anything, for how long, they did not know or care. Time was not a factor, the people around them who tried to break into their conversation didn't matter, and the waitress came and went. What mattered was that they were here together at last. Everything was natural, everything was fine.

Then, they were flying . . .

* * *

Kristie awoke with Brett on top of her. She held him close as she wiped some grit from her face. She did not remember much of the night, she must have had too many and invited Brett to come home with her. She could hear his breathing. It sounded odd. It sounded like a man who had just ran a race and now he was trying to catch his breath. Did they just have sex and she didn't remember it?

Then other sounds began to filter into to her cob webbed mind. Someone somewhere was crying. Suddenly she realized she was very cold even though, by the smell of it, there must have been a fire very near to her. Maybe she was just dreaming. She reached down to hug Brett closer to her. He felt cold as well except for a warm patch in middle of his back. It was wet.

Her eyes flew open. She remembered! They had been sent flying? But why? Earthquake! That must have been it; there had been no sound of an explosion. As if the Earth were affirming her guess, another temblor rumbled beneath them

Now the sounds around her became clearer. More people were crying and moaning. The first jolt must have been huge one and very near. She and Brett were under what as left of the patio's canvas canopy. They were both covered with dirt and stone. The stones must have come from the wall of the patio, the one that had the upper garden behind it.

She remembered it like a dream that happened long ago, but surely only minutes had passed. Her memories came back to her in slow motion. They had been talking, and then they were thrown up into the air by the great force of the quake. They were sailing through the air. She was looking at Brett, terrified, but he was not looking at her, his eyes were alive, assessing the situation around them even as they started the descent back to earth. What happened next could not have happened, but it must have, considering the position she and Brett were in now.

Her back had been to the garden wall. He must have seen something, because in mid-air he managed to force his body over her so she would be underneath him when they landed. They had hit the ground as everything came crashing down around and on top of them. Then darkness.

She was fully alert now and she had to get them out of there. The fire she smelled and now saw through the remains of the canopy must have been the burning bar. The smoke was getting thick as it became trapped under the heavy fabric that was covering them.

Still she did not panic. It was obvious that Brett was hurt and bleeding. She called to him to wake up.

"Brett. Can you here me? We have to move or we will suffocate."

He moaned. His eyes opened briefly and he smiled at her, blood covering his teeth. She smiled back.

"We have to move, Brett. The smoke from the fire is getting trapped under here; we will suffocate if we don't get out."

He did not seem to understand, as he made no move to free himself or her since she was trapped underneath him. So she began to squirm from side to side, in an attempt to wriggle free of his weight.

"Wait!"

It was Brett. Looking down at him, he now seemed fully awake, "There is something on my back. Let me lift up, so you can get out."

With that he moved his muscular arms into a position as if he were going to do a push up. He strained, started up, then fell back, momentarily knocking the wind out of Kristie. The smoke was getting thicker, faster now. Sensing the urgency, Brett heaved upward once more, this time making enough space so she could crawl out from under him. The edge of the tattered canopy was not far, so she scrambled to it and lifted it to let the air in. She called for Brett to follow her, but instead, he went down again. Looking around, she found a shattered beer bottle. She also saw what was on top of Brett. It was huge statue of Buddha that had adorned the upper garden. Brett must have seen that it was going to fall on her so he put himself between it and her fragile body.

He had saved her life.

Now, she had to save his. Frantically she slashed at the canvas that was trapping the stifling smoke. It took a few tries, but she managed to make a small tear in the material. After that, it split easily.

She tore it down to where Brett lay trapped under the weight of the heavy statue, a great plume of smoke billowed out, but she could hear Brett gasping for breath. He was still alive. He had managed to turn a little, so she was able to slide under the statue a little and hold him close to her. She had to keep him warm until help arrived. Looking around, she saw the wreckage of the bar and the patio. People lay motionless, some were moaning softly. Everything was destroyed. She began to cry.

She felt his hand come to her face. He was looking up at her smiling as best he could.

"Don't cry, Kristie. Everything will be alright."

His eyes were calm. The firelight put a glow in his deep brown eyes. He looked as if he had just wakened up from a restful sleep.

"I have to get you some help, Brett. You're hurt." she tried to hide the fear in her eyes as she looked at the huge red stain on the canvass. He was bleeding to death.

She started to get up, to cry out, and to get some help. She had to save him, but he held on to her.

"Stop, Kristie. Don't go. Stay with me, I'm not afraid."

"Don't talk like that, Brett. You will be okay. I have to go find some men to lift this statue off of you."

"Kristie, you won't find anyone—at least not it time." She looked wild eyed at him. He stroked her smudged cheek.

"I know this, Kristie. I know this. So stay with me for a little while longer." She wedged herself next to him again. Holding his head close to her breast. His breathing seemed less strained now and he was more relaxed. Then she felt a warm wetness soaking through the thin cloth of her blouse. Was he bleeding somewhere else? Looking down, she realized he was crying.

"I think I love you, Kristie. I think I have for a while now. I am glad that I had the chance to tell you." His arm circled her waist and hugged her closer to him.

"I love you too, Brett. When we get out of here, I will take you to my house and nurse you back to health. I will have you kicking and punching in no time, you'll see."

"I believe you, Kristie. When we get out of here . . ." his voice trailed off. She held him until his breathing stopped. Then she cursed him.

"Damn you, Brett. Damn you. Why did you have to die? It's easy for the dead. They just go off to where ever the dead go. It's we the living that have the hard part as we carry on with the wreckage of our lives."

As she held him closer, she was remorseful for her outburst.

"All the same, I still love you, I always will."

Then she kissed him good bye.

THE END

DREAM LOVERS

She stirred her coffee while looking absently out the window at the traffic on Main Street. No words were necessary now. The look that had passed between them was all the introduction that they required.

He sat opposite her, not uncomfortable, not happy, not any feeling that he could readily recognize, for it was a feeling that he had never encountered before. Her sleek body, her golden hair, her overly feminine features were just as he had seen them two nights before. No detail was out of place; not a hair was missed. He was amazed.

She turned back to him now, smiling, looking down as if afraid to meet his gaze, but no fear showed in her movements. Looking up, she spoke.

"You are just as I remembered. Am I a disappointment to you?"

"No. You are just as I remembered you as well. Maybe even more beautiful, if that is possible."

This brought a blush to her cheeks, "Do I look as good with my clothes on as I did with them off?"

"Of course. But don't make me out to be single-minded. Remember that we did many things outside of the bedroom. We went to Las Vegas for a week, to that wonderful resort, we spent the nights going from show to show, dancing, laughing, and holding hands. You looked fabulous in that slinky dress. Did you like it?"

"Yes. It was the kind of dress I always wanted to wear, cut down to the navel and laced in the middle. I never had the nerve to do it in real life. I was happy that you put me in it."

"It's funny", she went on, "but I remember seeing myself through your eyes. Could that be possible?"

"Is this possible? Is this happening? I feel wide-awake. Do you?"

"Yes it is and yes I am."

"Then it is possible. If this is possible, anything that happened two nights ago is possible."

"But I don't look like that. You gave me breast implants or something. And my hair! It was very nearly flaxen! Are my eyes really that blue?"

"Of course they are and you do look like that, you have just never seen yourself through the eyes of a lover."

"Do you suppose that was it?"

"I know it was, because I saw myself through your eyes."

This seemed to catch her off guard. For the first time she squirmed against the wicker seat of her chair. He felt her uneasiness and for a while quietly enjoyed it.

"Don't worry so. We all have our images of each other. I was glad you gave me so much hair—was it real or a toupee?—surgery maybe? And those pants! They were very tight, in just the right places. I would never feel comfortable walking around in them, even if I could fit into something like that."

Her face lit up with the memory. Her smile, in reality, was ever more radiant than he imagined.

"You do look like that. Sitting here, in what you are wearing, you look like that. You are very handsome."

"As you are beautiful, yes more beautiful than I remember."

Reaching out, their hands met. The spark that passed was electric, anyone in the City Bakery, who noticed, could tell they had been lovers. Wild, passionate, uncontrolled and unafraid lovers. Now they were here together, in the light of day for everyone to see.

As if this was perhaps more than they could bear so soon, they retreated from each other's touch. What they shared happened two days ago, this was now, and a lifetime, or possibly more, lay between them.

"How do you suppose it happened? How could we have met in a dream like that and then like this? Is this what people refer to as destiny?"

He looked thoughtful. In just the few minutes they had sat across from each other, his mind had conjured up many words: fate, karma, predestination, and a hundred other words men had tossed about in its search for an explanation of why things go as they do despite all of their exotic plans.

But of all of them he liked her word. Destiny. It was the most beautiful of all the words, it was appropriate that she had chosen it. It fit her so well.

"Destiny." he echoed, "I like the sound of that word. I just wish it was so, but I fear that it isn't. I fear that 'accidental' is the more appropriate word. No, don't look so sad. I am struggling not to. Although I am beginning to feel that way."

It was now her turn to be thoughtful; gazing into the coffee she had yet to take a drink of like a fortune teller looking into her glass orb as if the answers would suddenly crystallize and reveal the truth. She sat this way for some time before looking up. The faint wetness around her eyes revealed that the answers had not come; only the cold reality that was now quickly enveloping them both could be seen. They had precious little time left.

"Do you suppose", she asked, "that this is how it always is?"

"What do you mean?"

"Is this how it always is, the ones you meet in your dreams, are they always real people? Are they just in different parts of the world? Have they lived at different times? Were we never meant to meet them?"

She had paralleled his thoughts exactly. He was not surprised; she was, after all, a part of his life. For one lifetime, in a night, they had been soul mates, had been partners forever.

"I believe so. We are the accident, the exception to the rule. It may be just that we remember each other so well and because the time has been so short that is the difference. I know I have often met people who I thought I had met before. Perhaps they were all just apparitions, memories from the night, before the real world fleshed them out for me. I don't know for sure. I do know that if I had to meet any of them in any circumstance, I am happy that I met you, like this. You were special."

"As were you. Will—will we ever see each other again?"

"Of course." he said, rising to go home to his wife and children.

"I will see you in my dreams."

END

THE POWERS OF LOVE

Though his new form at first made it difficult, Elvin moved quickly to clean up the mess he had made. His thrashing about during the transformation had caused a few vials and vases to be knocked down, spilling their contents. His clothes, now much to small for him, had split at the seams to become rags on the floor. He used them to wipe up the liquids.

He pulled on some of the Sorcerer's own clothes, which Elvin had the foresight to hide in a cabinet under his master's workbench. He had put them there, long before, hoping to some day possess the time—and audacity—to carry out the mission he had just completed. Then again, he had always been a great deal more intelligent, and driven, than people had credited him to be.

Just because he was an orphan, he was often pitied and perceived as being wretched. Although Elvin hated this assumption people placed upon him, in the end, he realized that had it not been for being thought of as such he would not be in the position that he now found himself. Baldor the Sorcerer, feeling sorry for him, had taken him from a life of begging on the streets to be his apprentice—a very noble profession for anyone.

With the mess now cleaned up and everything put back as he had encountered them, he had time to look at the man he had created. Gazing downward upon himself he evaluated the product of his own private sorcery.

He was now approximately 75 inches standing and roughly 12 stone in weight. Though he approved of his work, at the same time he knew that his actions would be his death if he did not act quickly. Still, if forfeiting his short life meant he could spend just one minute locked in passion with Katelin then he would gladly give it away.

The thought of her warmth and beauty spurred him out the door of the workshop to venture upon the second part of his feverishly assembled plan.

*　　*　　*

Outside he found himself the target of great many stares. Men huddled in doorways as he strode by. He knew they were murmuring questions about his presence. Elvin was positive that none suspected him to be the small child he had been just the hour before, no they questioned the sight of a stranger, especially such a large stranger, in their midst.

Their curiosity made him move forward even more briskly. Not only did he not desire to rouse too much suspicion, he also yearned for Katelin to look upon him as many of the young ladies he now passed looked upon him. Their longing gazes made him realize that he had not just changed in size; he was now handsome as well. The thought warmed his heart.

His great strides brought him quickly to Katelin's courtyard then to her door on which he knocked vigorously, while calling out to her.

Finally, the door cracked a hand span. Mauden, her faithful chambermaid looked out; her face defiant against anyone who would disturb the peace of her homestead.

"Who is it that wishes to see Lady Katelin?"

"Tis I Mauden, Elvin. I have come to see the Lady today as I have in many days past.

The door closed, abruptly.

"You must call her, Mauden. I can explain, but only to her. Only she will know that I speak the truth."

The door cracked again.

"Master Elvin is a child. You are a man. Now go away."

Knowing that time was his enemy Elvin gently, but firmly, pushed his way inside the house. This sent Mauden scuttling towards the sewing room, one of Katelin's favorite places this time of day.

A commotion ensued that brought forth Katelin, Mauden, and Hester, the ancient family man servant. The trio stood together in defiance of the large man who had invaded their domain. All looked frightened.

"Do not fear me! I am Elvin. I came here just two days past as I had come many times before. Katelin, you must believe me. You must also know now that I am in grave danger. Please, come with me. We must flee."

Katelin, her face a mix of fear and confusion stood her ground.

"What have you done with the boy? How did you persuade him to tell you of his visits? If you have harmed him in anyway his master, Baldor, will be upon you like a vulture on carrion. He loves that boy."

"No, no, Katelin. He does not! Yes he tolerated me, but he does not love me. Besides, his feelings are of no matter between us. I love you, I have always loved you. That is why I come to you this way. That is why I have put my life in danger. I desired you to see me not just as a boy, but as a man."

Now anger, real anger, flared in her eyes. She turned and seized a slightly rusted sword that hung on the wall of her entryway. With speed and skill he had never seen in her before, she thrust the tip under Elvin's chin before he could take a step back.

"You would kill me? After all I have risked coming to you as I am now?"

"I would kill any stranger who burst upon me and mine so."

Desperately, Elvin pleaded, "But I am no stranger. I am who I say I am. I can prove it."

The tip of the sword wavered slightly.

"How so?"

Elvin's eyes looked to Mauden then Hester, reluctant to speak in front of them. Katelin seemed to sense this.

"Speak what you will. I have no secrets from these two. If you are who you say you are you know that they are family to me. The only family I have left."

"Yes, Katelin. In my panic I have forgotten."

"Then speak or die." The sword tip once more steadied against his throat.

"A stranger would not know that you were to have a child Katelin. A child by a man whom you never identified, but a man you said could never marry you. To have the child would have been a disgrace to your family name, but you would have loved it no matter what the consequences. Unfortunately, the child died in a premature birth leaving you with mixed emotions of redress and grief. When I first came to you as a messenger for my master, you took to me as if I was that dead child, now born whole. You invited me back as my time spared. And I did come back, repeatedly over the years. First I came as an orphaned child seeking his mother, but as I grew older, I came as man seeking his soul mate."

The sword dropped to her side, then clanged to the floor. Katelin seemed to sway, causing Hester to put forth a hand to steady her. After a moment, she turned to her domestic companions and asked that they leave. Reluctantly, they both turned to go eyeing the mysterious stranger who spoke such truths as they went.

Just as they left the room, the door burst open behind him. Elvin did not need the look of terror on Katelin's face to know that his death, and possibly hers, had just entered the room.

"So my assumptions were correct Elvin?"

Elvin stooped quickly to pick up the sword from the ground where it had fallen. He was no longer a child; he would fight as man would fight, no matter what the odds were against his survival.

As he spun to face his new enemy, a great laugh burst forth from the sorcerer's lips.

"I see you are thinking like a man as well as looking like one now, Elvin. Yet, this is how you would repay me for my kindness? You would bear arms against the man who saved you from the gutters? The man who taught you to read and write in times of great illiteracy? Such is not the gratitude of a man Elvin. Such is the ingratitude of a child too young to realize what has been bestowed upon him."

Elvin wavered for a moment. "I do not bear arms against the man you describe Baldor. I bear arms against the man who would come to stop me in my quest."

This brought forth another great guffaw from Baldor's lips. After a while his fit or merriment passed turning his look into pity as he scrutinized Elvin.

"No son, I do not wish to stop you, but stop you I must even if it means your death. For you now have secrets that are not to be trusted in the hands of ordinary men. Fashioning grown men from children is a dark art that many Kings would pay handsomely to have. I cannot be positive that you could resist the kinds of temptations they would lay before you. Had you stayed with me, going from a child to a man in the way that all children grow, I may have come to trust you with these secrets. But to come upon them this way, through deception, cannot be allowed."

Elvin lunged toward his Master.

Baldor shouted a word. His hand raised and fell, the room became a blaze of light, and then Elvin could move no more!

Behind him, he heard Katelin cry out. He would have cried himself had he been capable of doing so. Before him, he could see his out stretched arm and the sword within his hand; both had turned a pasty white. He tried to move his head but his body would not, could not, do that which his mind asked it to do.

Katelin, sobbing, moved between himself and Baldor.

"What sorcery is this, you monster? What have you done to Elvin?"

"I merely stopped him from killing me. Would you expect me to do otherwise? Fear not though Lady Katelin, he is not dead. He lives; he hears each word said between us. He will remain so until I deem otherwise."

"This is not living Baldor. You have transformed him into a statue! To be like this and to be alive at the same time is worse than death."

As the weight of her words fell on his ears, Elvin shuddered, or would have shuddered had be been capable of doing so. The thought of being entombed as he was for eternity was indeed a fate far worse than death.

"Fear not my Lady. He will not stay as such. I will only keep him so only until I have decided on how to handle his insolence. You seem to forget that I love the boy. Any other man would be dead by now!

Nevertheless, how shall I keep what he knows from spreading to others? True, I can easily change him back into the shape he once was, but that would not purge his memory. Perhaps I should make him an imbecile who would be incapable of keeping thoughts in his head? No, then he would be of no use to me. Taking his gift of speech would not stop him since he knows how to write.

Blinding him would still leave him capable of speech. No, this is a dilemma that will take some time to sort out. Until I do, he can remain as he is."

Katelin turned to Elvin. Looking into his pasty eyes, she put a hand he could not feel to his cheek.

"You must not punish him Baldor. Punish me instead. It is for I that he betrayed you."

Baldor thought about this for a moment. "Nay Lady Katelin, you are not the wrong doer here. True, you are the inspiration, but you are not the perpetrator. Then again, young Elvin here is not the first man-boy to risk his life for the love of a beautiful woman. So, that being said, it must be love and desire that is in the wrong here."

Baldor closed his great eyes for a moment as if contemplating the words he had just spoken.

"Stand back Lady Katelin. Your words have inadvertently made me realize what I must do."

"Then he will live like any other man, Baldor?"

"Mostly, yes he will. He will no longer be a statue and I shall return him to the boy he once was, but he will no longer be a full man. I have decided that I must make him incapable of feeling love for anyone or anything from this day forward. By dousing these flames in his soul, he will not hunger for the touch of another. He will no longer be tempted to aspire to things greater than his own being for the sake of the love of another."

Katelin's hand flew to her speechless mouth. Baldor raised his hands, manipulating his fingers in a complex dance of sorcery. He chanted words that she could not understand.

Even in his tomb-like condition, Elvin realized what was about to happen. His eyes fixed on the back of Katelin's head. He remembered how soft her flaxen hair felt when he braided it for her. He remembered her smell of honeysuckle and the soft touch of her skin. His heart pounded feverishly within his chest as grief came over him. He wanted to remember her later as he knew her now, but after Baldor finished his work; he realized that he would never know her that way again. Why did Baldor not just strike him dead! He would have much preferred that fate to the one that was planned for him now.

In front of him, Katelin regained her gift of communication and once more began to plead with Baldor to end his chanting. Her words did not faze the Sorcerer. Finally, as the old man looked upward, Katelin lunged at him, striking him full in the chest with all of her weight.

They both tumbled roughly to the stone floor where they lay momentarily dazed. Baldor attempted to get up first. Seeing this, Katelin flung herself violently upon him, pinning him to the old man to the ground with surprising strength.

"No. You will not finish Baldor. You will listen to me. I have a way to end this madness with no harm to you or the boy. You must listen."

At her words, Baldor stopped struggling. Katelin slid from him.

"Speak Lady."

Looking back at Elvin, she pulled the old man to him and whispered feverishly in his ear.

Baldor looked up at Elvin when she finished, "You would do this for the boy?"

"If it is possible, yes."

"It is possible. Come with me."

With that, they both left Elvin's line of sight, apparently retreating to an adjoining room.

A few minutes later, only Baldor emerged. He began another incantation, waved his hands, and caused smoke to fill the room once more.

Elvin found himself on the floor, a small child once more, looking up at old Baldor. Nowhere was Katelin to be found. He rushed at the Sorcerer, striking out wildly.

"What have you done with Katelin? Did you kill her? I will kill you someday, somehow if you harmed her."

"Hold back boy! She is well. Except for the fact that she seems to love you more than anything in the world. Look behind you."

As he turned, Elvin saw the most beautiful little girl he had ever known come out the room where Baldor had been. Her hair was flaxen, she smelled of honeysuckle, and her skin was a smooth as that of a newborn child.

She spoke, "Tis I Elvin. Tis I Katelin."

"But . . ."

"Fear not Elvin. I've come to no harm. I am just as I was when I was child. Now I shall go with you back to Baldor's house. We shall grow up together in the way all children grow. We will have our love for longer than even you had planned on and Baldor will now have another assistant."

Tears rolled down Elvin's face.

"You have done this for me? Then you love me as I love you?"

"Yes Elvin, I love you."

Behind them, Baldor cleared his throat.

"Come now children we must be getting back. There is work to be done— the King is waiting!"

With that, he turned to leave, muttering as he went about the mysterious powers of love.

Behind him, two children walked hand and hand into their future.

THE END

THE RIGHT NOTE

"You play the Cello, don't you?"

Sandra whirled around to see who was making the inquiry of her. She found herself looking at a short man (though he was about her own height), broad in the shoulder and thick in his chest. His arms bulged under the thin black T-shirt he was wearing. His stomach had the swelling of a man just entering his middle ages. His face was "nice", not overtly handsome, nor ugly. He surely did not look like a music critic. She turned away ignoring him, hoping that he would go away—or speak to her again.

"I saw you perform last night at the Sherman Performing Arts Center. My son was in the chorale that sang during the performance of *Beethoven's 9th Symphony*."

She turned back, intrigued now. The chorale that performed last night was a aggregation of several choirs from local colleges. That meant that the man had a son of college age. He did not look old enough, she thought bitterly. It also meant that he was married.

"You managed to see me among the hundred and eleven people in the orchestra?"

"Yes", he said.

"You must have been sitting up close."

"I was in the 10th row on the other side of the stage from you. Most of the time you were hidden behind that older cellist, but yes, I was able to pick you out. I guess it was the dress you were wearing or the way you were playing. You stood out to me."

Sandra thought about the frumpy way she looked this Sunday morning compared to last night. She had been wearing her, semi-short black dress, thin spiked black heels, and a single strand of pearls. It all contrasted her, still natural, shiny blonde hair. Though she felt the outfit made her look fantastic, it was not much different than what many of the other women around her wore. So, what was this man's game? She decided to call him on it.

"Did your wife enjoy the show?"

"I will ask her the next time I see her. She was there last night, of course, with her new boyfriend. I am not sure she was paying a lot of attention, though."

Her heart was buoyed at his response.

"You don't mind your wife going out with other men?"

"Not as long as when she signs our final divorce papers she doesn't hit me up for alimony. I don't care who she sees. It wouldn't matter to her anyway if I did."

Did Sandra see a slight touch of emotion around his eyes as he made this last statement? Was it real? It looked real to her.

"Well, I am glad you liked the performance. I can't say that I added much more than anyone of the other cellists around me, but thank you for noticing me."

"How could I not? Your eyes were ablaze with feeling; you almost seemed as if you were not on stage but playing your instrument from high above the auditorium while letting the notes cascade down around the ears of the listeners. You were a gracious goddess sharing your heavenly gifts with all those present."

Was this man a poet?

"Sorry. That was the writer in me slipping out. I usually keep him reined in while in the supermarket. I guess there is just something about you that brings that out in me. As I watched you last night, I had an idea for a story and I was up past 2 AM this morning working on it. Secretly I hoped that, someday, you would be able to read it, but I never really expected to see you again."

Was this just a line? If it was, it was not one Sandra had heard before. He sounded genuine enough, and now there was no mistaking the emotion—and gentle kindness—that showed in his deep brown eyes. Still, as much as she hoped he was for real, she could never be sure.

"Well, maybe someday I will." she said demurely, not wanting to be unkind.

"Then I can see you again?"

Uh-oh . . .

"Um, sure. We are performing next Friday in Oakmont at the philharmonic hall. You can see me then." she replied, unable to suppress a shy smile.

He smiled in return.

"Okay then, it's a date. I will see you on Friday."

As he turned to walk away, Sandra felt a pang of regret. Had she been too abrupt? She really would not mind seeing this stranger again. Maybe they could be friends. She wondered who he was.

As if reading her mind, he turned back to her and said, "Dalton. Brian David Dalton."

With a wave and a laugh, he disappeared around the corner of the aisle.

*　　*　　*

Sandra scanned the audience. Something she never did during a performance. Would Brian be here? She felt she could use his first name since she had spent a good part of the last week with "him", or at least with the words that he wrote.

It took some searching, first in the local library then on the Internet, but she managed to find two stories he had written. She was surprised to see that they were tender love stories. One was a very short surrealistic work about two lovers who meet in a dream then meet in real life, the other was a long, adventurous tale set in the old west about a man who goes looking for treasure and finds true love. She was touched by the compassion exhibited in each story.

For the past few days she had resisted the urge to try to contact him, great though it was. She did not want to seem too eager and maybe scare him off nor did she want to jump into a relationship with a man who apparently had just ended a marriage. She was not looking to be a rebound. She had caught one of them after her own failed marriage and that turned out to be a disaster.

The footlights made it impossible to see the first 10 rows, so if he was here, he was up close. Despite the fact that the theater seated over 2500 people, she was confident that she could have picked him out had she been able to spot him; his face was etched in her memory and became ever more so with each of his words that she read.

The evening's performance of Tchaikovsky's *Symphony 6 Pathetique* seemed flat and impassive to her ears. She played the notes on the page, but her mind and emotions were not there. This drew a few concerned looks from the Maestro who had conducted her in past and knew of her zeal. Afterwards he asked if she was feeling well. She lied about having a slight headache as she packed up to go to her car.

"You seemed a little lackluster tonight?" said a familiar voice as she stepped out the stage door.

He was standing in the circle of light projected by the lamp above the door. He was dressed in a tuxedo, with a white tie and crimson cummerbund. She barely recognized him.

"Yes," Sandra replied, "I suppose I was. Not every night will be a winner, I am fortunate to have excellent performers backing me up. So, why are you here?"

"Remember our date?"

Pushy wasn't he? She had a mind to tell him off, but of course, she could not.

"I thought you were teasing." she replied.

"No, I was very sincere. I know this is forward of me, but I had hoped you would at least patronize my foolishness. After seeing you perform, I greatly wanted to meet you and talk to you about your music. Running into you in the store last week was pure fortune; I promise that I am not stalking you. I don't even know your name."

She was touched by his honesty and sincerity. His use of the word fortune seemed very appropriate as well.

She smiled and held out her hand, "Brian David Dalton meet Sandra Angela Foster."

His hand was warm and dry. His grip was firm but not confining.

"A pleasure, Sandra. I know it is late, but would you join me for a drink?"

"Yes I will, but I have to take my car," she half lied, "I can't just leave my instrument in a dark, empty parking lot."

"Of course." Brian replied as he took her case from her hand, "Lead the way."

As they walked along they chatted about the night's performance, the weather, and anything else that did not really concern the two of them a great deal. After they loaded up her instrument, she drove him to his car, which turned out to be an old Buick Skylark that looked brand new. He called it his "classic".

She followed him to hotel bar not far from the performing arts center. The thought of the lounge being in a hotel only scared her a little, after all, she was all grown up now.

Finding a table and ordering drinks, a scotch and soda for him, a strawberry daiquiri for her, they settled into a long talk.

She told him how she had taken up the cello when she was seven years old, not revealing how long ago that had been, despite her father wanting her to follow him into his accounting firm. She had never had an affinity for mathematics in a paper and pencil way, but she loved the mathematics involved in music. She could hear and feel them much better than she could ever visualize them. Her mother, who had performed a little in college theater understood this and supported her even when she was struggling to find a paid position in an orchestra so she could make her rent each month.

She had married the lead violinist who seemed charming and kind, but who turned out to be vain and cruel. They had divorced after eleven years of a noisy marriage and for the past six years, she had not really dated anyone on a steady basis.

Brian was just the opposite. He had married his high school sweetheart and started a career in the construction trade, eventually owning his own contractor business. He started writing as a way to pass the time while recovering from a back injury that laid him up for months. He had been surprised at how easy the work came to him since he only dreamed of writing in the past. When he sold his first story to an Internet based magazine for $5.00, he was thrilled— even though they never got around to paying him.

Over the course of a twenty-five year marriage, that produced just one son, he found that he was growing and changing while his wife stayed the naïve high school girl that he fell in love with. Year by year, they grew apart. Finally, since his son was a grown man now, he decided to get out of the marriage. He still ran his business, but his chronic back injury kept him from doing a lot of the work he enjoyed. So, he hired others to run his job sites and he stayed home and wrote. His son worked for him occasionally as school permitted. Brian was hoping that his son would not get too interested in construction and would continue his pursuit of a degree in International Business.

"Do you only write love stories?" Sandra asked before she realized what she was saying.

He looked astonished.

"So you have read some of my stories?" he said, softly taking her hand.

She hoped he did not see her blushing in the low light of the bar.

"Well, I was a little curious after our odd encounter in the store. I had to look you up and see if you were famous or not."

"Were you disappointed?"

"Not with your status—or your stories. You write magnificently. I am sure that someday you will be discovered to be a great author."

"Maybe after I am dead." he said with a cheerless smile, "Sometimes I think that is why I write. So when I do die, a little part of me will go on forever, or at least as long as anyone remembers my work. I mean, is Shakespeare really dead? Have any of the masters, whose music you play so well, really departed this Earth? I say no, not as long as people remember their works. As long as they exist in a thought, they will be immortal. I suppose I wish to join their company some day."

Sandra continued to be amazed and touched by this man!

"I agree—writers are immortalized in the written word, like artists in their paintings and composers in their music. All creativeness is immortalized, if not in the tangible sense, then in its affect upon people who in turn, affect other people exponentially forward through time."

Again he looked astonished.

"That was a beautiful thought, Sandra, very well expressed. Have you ever considered writing?"

"No, but maybe I will start. Will you help me find a publisher?" she squeezed his hand.

"Of course I will, Sandra" he said leaning close to her.

They both felt a little embarrassed at their sudden intimacy.

Sandra sat up slightly, smiling shyly.

"Is this the part where you say something about me having something more exciting between my legs besides a cello? I mean is that why we are in a hotel bar?"

"I must have left that line in the puerile mind of the teenager I was once long ago," he said smiling back at her, "but as a grown man, I admit having thought about it after we sat down in here."

"Afterwards? Not before?"

"No. Not before."

"I am not sure if I should feel insulted or flattered." her grin widened.

"Just be happy, Sandra. As happy as I am right now." Brian leaned forward and kissed her tenderly.

Sandra sat back after a while.

"Should we inquire about a room for the night? I want to even though I don't know you well."

Brian looked solemn for a few minutes as if he were fighting devils inside him.

"Not tonight, Sandra. Most of me wants to, but I think we might be better off waiting, at least for a while."

"Of course, Brian. We can wait, we have time."

"Yes," he replied, "We have eternity ahead of us."

THE END

THE LAST ROAD TRIP

"**H**e's gone!"

Sarah looked up from the Daily Paid Claims chart she was perusing to see Catherine standing in her cubicle looking pale and shaken. Immediately, she stood up and helped her into a chair. Catherine's skin was cold to her touch.

"Catherine, you look ill! Can I get you some water, coffee maybe?"

She shook her head as she sat down, and then laid it in her arms folded across Sarah's desk. She murmured again, "He's gone!"

"Who Catherine? Who is gone?" asked Sarah, starting to feel afraid.

"Jack—he's gone. He left me a some—some things; I know he's gone."

"Jack? You mean my Jack or Jack Curtis out in the call center?" Sarah knew that Catherine was friends with both.

"'Your' Jack." she said with a hint of spite in her voice.

Sarah, puzzled by Catherine's tone, walked to the door of her cubicle and saw that Jack Marner's chair was indeed empty. Her digital watch read 1:59 PM, too late for him to be at lunch since he always, like clockwork, went at noon. It was only then she realized that she had not seen Jack all day. She had been in and out of meetings all morning and even on days she was not, his quiet nature sometimes made him seem invisible. Yet for him to not be here at all, as Catherine seemed certain of, without giving her a call, was as unheard of event—especially on a Monday, the call center's busiest day of the week.

"Catherine," she said soothingly, placing a hand on her shoulder, "I'm sure he is just out on the units helping one of the associates. You know how they call on him for everything and how he always goes no matter what."

"Yes, I know. But he's not out on the units; I just looked out there for him. He's gone." she replied holding out a small stack of paper she had brought with her. "He left me this."

Sarah looked at the documents Catherine handed them to her. The first page appeared to be the cover page of a manuscript. Not unusual since Jack was a writer and often shared his stories with the staff. The page read: *The Last Road Trip* by Jack Marner. It sounded interesting. For a moment Sarah forgot Catherine's discomfort and wished that she could read the work. She enjoyed her assistant's writing and always thought that someday he would be successful. That would mean he would leave her—and the company, of course. She suppressed a sigh.

Looking back at Catherine, who seemed to be on the edge of tears, she sat down next to her.

"What is it that has upset you, Catherine? Did Jack say he was leaving? I mean, is he gone for good? Did he . . . did he quit?" the last was almost a whisper.

"No, he didn't 'quit' in the way you think." Catherine snapped at Sarah, sitting up straight in her chair. She hated Sarah's possessiveness of Jack. She always to clung to him, but she never really knew him. Often times, when Jack was in one of his many gloomy moods, Sarah would ask Catherine what was bothering him instead of asking Jack himself.

Sarah didn't care for Catherine's tone. After all she was just another assistant like Jack, while Sarah had worked her way up from the sales floor to become a Company Director "Then tell me what you are talking about. Your not just being overly emotional are you? I mean, I know how you feel about Jack."

"When I leave, you can look over those pages. You might be able to tell from it that he is gone, but you won't know where or why because I know he never confided in you. I know what those words mean, I know where he is going, and what he is going to do.", Catherine began to quietly weep.

Suddenly the manuscript in Sarah's hands felt like it weighed a hundred pounds. Her arms strained under what she knew was the truth in Catherine's statement. She wanted to drop them on the floor, throw them in the trash, or feed them to "Anderson" her small shredder. It was Jack who gave the machine its cute nickname.

At the same time, she wanted to sit and read what Jack had written, but that would mean ignoring Catherine, and right now she felt she should listen to what the young lady had to say. She sat down opposite from Catherine and held her hand as the girl slowly pulled herself together.

"Tell me about Jack, Catherine."

"He's gone. He won't be coming back. He's going to kill himself."

Sarah felt a dampness fall upon her. She understood why Catherine's skin felt cold; it was as if someone left the door open and the morning fog had drifted in.

Catherine was struck by the look on Sarah's face. She looked as if she had seen the end of her own life. Had there been something between Jack and Sarah? Probably only in Sarah's mind she concluded, otherwise Jack would have said something to her. Besides, she knew that there was only one woman for Jack—a woman he said he could never have. He probably could have had Sarah at anytime even though she was married, with children.

"Your just guessing." Sarah finally blurted out, it was a hiss.

"I knew him better than you did, Sarah", she replied, not aware of her use of the past tense. "He is going to kill himself."

"Why?" Sarah cried. Tears began to well up in her deep blue-eyes as she remembered how Jack once noticed how beautiful they were. It was the only compliment he had ever paid her.

Catherine wondered if she should tell Sarah? The whole ordeal would be bad enough as it is, since it was now apparent to her that Sarah had deeply loved Jack. Maybe if she knew, if she understood, how inevitable it all was, maybe then she would feel better.

"Don't cry Sarah. He is not doing it because of you or me. He must have finally gotten tired of carrying his burden. I honestly don't know how he bore it this long. I would have crumbled beneath it's weight a long time ago."

"Is—is he sick? Is that why he wants to kill himself?"

"Not 'sick' in the way you are probably thinking, Sarah, but sick in a way that has plagued men for as long as they have been on Earth."

Not understanding, Sarah said, "But I can get him help! I know hundreds of doctors from my work here, they are best there are. I will get him cured and I will pay for it all. We have to find him and help him."

Sarah stood, glancing around her cubicle as if she were looking for a magic potion that would ease her pain and cure the man she loved. Spying the phone, she picked it up. "I am calling the police."

"No!" shouted Catherine.

"No", speaking softer now, "That is the last thing he wants. Besides, knowing Jack it is much too late for that, he doesn't want to be stopped, so he won't be." She gently took the phone from Sarah's hand and put it back in it's cradle.

Sarah sat down meekly recognizing the truth in Catherine's words. She picked up the sheets of paper, gazing blankly at the pages.

"You don't have to read that, Sarah. I'll tell you what is in those pages."

Sarah nodded dumbly at Catherine, waiting for her next words.

"That isn't a story, at least not one that Jack wrote. It is a story, though, in that he assembled a song list and the lyrics, which he included in there, make up a story for those who understand their meaning. It took a while, but I finally understood that the time he told me about has arrived."

Sarah wanted to shout, but she did not, "He told you he wanted to kill himself? Why didn't you tell me? We could have called Employee Assistance. They would have counseled him."

"He never told he me he wanted to kill himself, Sarah. He just mentioned to me a few times that he knew that he would die by his own hand. He said he realized this since he was a teenager. While he was in college, he studied some faddish psychoanalytic technique and through that he determined that, someday, he would take his own life, I never paid this revelation much mind even though I knew that for the past year he was miserable most of the time."

Sarah looked puzzled; what could these pages have revealed to Catherine? She turned to the second page in the stack of papers she held as if in the truth would be written there. What she saw was a neatly typed and numbered song list. Very organized, just like Jack:

It read:

1. A Girl Like You
2. Wouldn't It Be Nice
3. God Only Knows
4. Higher Love
5. Breakfast At Tiffany's
6. Come Sail Away
7. Only A Memory
8. Twenty Nine Palms
9. Comfortably Numb
10. Viva Las Vegas
11. Black
12. Alone Again, Naturally

"I will bring you the CD he burned for me with those songs on it after we talk. You can listen to the words. As you do, then you will know that I am right. They convinced me."

Sarah was familiar with most of the songs, and knew the words to many of them. It pleased her in an odd way, despite the circumstances, that Jack would use some songs that were favorites of hers. They had never talked about music.

Catherine pulled her chair around to Sarah's side of the desk. She put her arm gently on the older woman's shoulder and gave her a tender hug.

"Sarah, Jack was crazy in love with a woman who works here." Sarah's eyes brightened for a moment. "I don't think it was you, though." Catherine added, trying to be gentle.

"He never told me who it was, but he would tell me about her and sometimes he would cry because he knew she could never be his. She is a very happily married woman. A fact that pleased him in some small way."

"It could have been me.", Sarah lied, not wanting to get into how miserable her own marriage had become.

"I don't think so, Sarah. Did you ever bake for him?"

"No. Why? Is that important? Should I have baked him something?"

"No, I don't believe that would not have changed anything. But the woman he was so desperately in love with did bake something for him. I came in one day to find that he was actually happy. He was smiling and he gave me a big hug. I asked him why he was so cheerful and he told me that his special friend had baked him two blueberry muffins. He said blueberry was his favorite kind, and he said he had never told her this. It was as if he were telling me again how right they would be for each other."

"She sounds very special." said Sarah.

"More special to him than anyone he'd ever met, Sarah. I often wished someone would love me like Jack loved her. Did he ever let you read a story of his called *I Know Why?*"

Sarah shook her head in response.

"I have a copy of it. He made me promise to not let anyone else read it, ever. He made me promise this because he thought that someone might recognize the character in the story and guess who she was, though I never did. Still, he didn't want to start any rumors because he didn't want to cause the woman any trouble. But, I think now that he wouldn't mind, I think he would want you to understand and I know you wouldn't tell any of it to anyone if you can figure out who the character is supposed to be."

"I would like to read it, Catherine. I want to understand."

"Okay, just have plenty of tissues nearby when you do. Though the end turns out happy, in getting there you read a tale of a man possessed. One who can't eat, sleep, or do anything without having the woman in his mind. It is so much more sad now because I know now that the happy ending he wrote about will never happen."

Tears streamed down both of the women's faces. They turned and held each other for a moment. Sarah's two girls were both just children, but she often hoped that they would both grow up to be sweet, hard-working women in the mold of Catherine.

Catherine picked up the sheets of paper Sarah had laid down.

"In *A Girl Like You* a man is saying he would do anything or say anything to be with the woman he loves. I know Jack wouldn't do that in this case because, as I said, he never wanted to complicate the life of this woman. But I know he burned to tell her; this is the burden he bore everyday since he met her about a year ago."

"Yes," Sarah replied pointing to the list, "and in *Wouldn't It Be Nice* he is saying how badly he wanted to be with her all the time. I remember thinking that about a boy I liked when I first heard it."

For a moment her mind drifted back to those innocent, virginal days, wishing she were there instead of here facing what she now realized were the grim reality of Catherine's word. She went on in a dreamy haze, "*God Only Knows* shows the enormous depth of his love—as if no human could ever fully understand it. It makes me realize why he would be miserable all the time, as you say he was."

Catherine agreed smiling in a way that she hoped eased Sarah's pain.

"He told me that he had no idea that he, or anyone else, could love someone so much. He couldn't even express it in words, which is why he must have added *Higher Love*. It must have come as close as he could ever imagine the words would be if he could only write them."

"*Breakfast At Tiffany's* seems out of place, even though it is a wonderful song and one of my favorites."

"I think I understand that one. He once told me that his mystery woman was a perfect match for him. They had so much in common with each other including the kind of movies they like."

"Clever!" Sarah said, momentarily remembering the words to the song while forgetting why she and Catherine were looking at the list. When she remembered, tears started to flow once more.

Catherine gave her a few minutes to compose herself.

"If it makes it any better, I felt the same way after I saw the list. He *was* a clever man, so there is no need to be sad just because we recognize that. It is just one more of the reasons why we loved him."

Sarah appreciated the truth in this statement. She turned back to the list.

"*Come Sail Away* tells he is us he is leaving, leaving the Earth. He is telling us that he will be going off somewhere to a place he has never been to with beings the likes of he has never met before." she stated.

"Of course." Catherine agreed, "*Only A Memory* tells us that his would-be lover will soon only be just a remembrance to him. The inclusion of *Twenty Nine Palms* had me stumped for a while until I listened closely to the haunting lyrics."

"Tell me what he meant by that one."

"Did you know that he liked to go to Las Vegas? He went almost every weekend."

Sarah shook her head. There seemed to be much that she did not know about "her" Jack.

"Well after I listened more closely to the words, I remembered that he told me liked to listen to one particular radio station while he was driving across the desert. The station is located in Twenty Nine Palms, California. That song showed me that he was going over there now. *Comfortably Numb* tells me that, as he drives over there for the last time, he is going to try to put her out of his mind for good. He will try to make himself deadened to the feelings of love for her so he won't back out of what he thinks he must do. He must end his life so he won't be so miserable all the time. I think he finally realized that he would never get over her as long as he was alive."

"Maybe not Catherine! He might just be moving there to get away from her. We could probably find him if he is.", Sarah said hopefully.

"That would be nice to think, but the next three songs seem to say otherwise."

Sarah frowned at this. Tears started rolling down her cheeks once more.

"*Viva Las Vegas* makes it obvious that he going there to have one last wild fling. *Black* tells a moving, tragic story of a man who is in love with a woman that he cannot have. He finally comes to the realization that the woman will end up making someone happy, but he also knows that 'someone' will never be him."

The final haunting refrains of the song had played in Catherine's mind ever since she realized what all this meant. It was a soaring, relentless, climax of pain and self-realization. The singer sounded out the agony that must have been in Jack's heart.

"Of course *Alone Again, Naturally* talks about suicide and abject loneliness." Sarah whispered; at that moment she could not remember a time when she felt so wretched.

"There is tower somewhere in Las Vegas—"

"I know the one; I have been there." Sarah murmured.

"I think that is where he going to do it. He is going to the top and fall off of it."

"'Fall' off of it?"

"Yes, Sarah. Remember that. We can never let anyone know what we suspect and we don't know the truth for sure, anyway. See, if he jumps off in an obvious act of suicide, his son would not get the proceeds of his life insurance, but if he makes it look like an accident, then the company will have to pay off. Maybe his son could even sue the place if Jack makes the 'accident' look as if negligence was involved. Most likely he will just get drunk and somehow go over the side. My feeling is that he has done this already."

Sarah was insensate. Jack dead? Already? That would be like him. It would also be like him to make sure someone knew that he was acting in a rational manner even in the wake of an irrational emotion. In one way, she was glad that she knew whatever it was she did know, since she could help him in his final wish. For the next few days she would monitor the news for stories of Jack's death. She would also report him as being missing from his job and most likely having abandoned it. Then any actions taken by Human Resources— even the pay out of a company life insurance policy—would come across Sarah's desk since she was his last Supervisor. She would make sure the money would go to his son. She was sure Jack had already made these arrangements, but she would be there just to ensure they took place.

"Are you all right?" Catherine asked.

Sarah nodded. No words could come to her at the moment.

"Okay. I am going back to my desk. I don't know if I can work anymore today, but I have to at least look like I am doing something."

Sarah liked Catherine. She wondered if Catherine would consider coming to work for her now that Jack would not be with her anymore?

"You be okay." Catherine said. It was a statement.

She forced a smile as she turned and walked out of Sarah's cubicle feeling sorry for the older woman's grief on one hand while trying to deal with her own on the other.

As she was wandering idly back to her desk, just getting one foot to follow the other, Catherine heard someone humming a familiar tune. She followed the sound.

It brought her to the cubicle of one of the many clerks employed by her company. She had on a set of headphones, apparently humming along with the sound in her ears. Seeing Catherine staring at her, she slowly slipped the headphones down around her neck.

Catherine had met the lady once before when she started to work here about a year ago, but could not now remember her name.

"Um, what are you listening to?" she asked in a silly little girl kind of voice, feeling embarrassed as she did so. The lady would probably think she was a simpleton.

To the contrary, though, she flashed a brilliant smile that lit up her pale blue eyes in such way it even made Catherine's heart jump.

"Oh, just any little thing." the lady responded in a sultry tone. Catherine remembered that she spoke in this manner.

"Do you want to hear it?" she asked, reaching to unplug the headphones so her speakers would issue the music.

"No. That's okay, but I know the song you were humming. Someone left a CD on my desk with that same song on it."

This brought a puzzled smile to the lady's face.

"Isn't that strange, sugar? Somebody left this CD on my desk, too. Do you suppose we have a secret admirer?" she said as she flashed her sparkling smile again.

Catherine's heart leapt once more at the sheer brilliance of it; it matched the shine coming off the huge gold and diamond band that was wrapped around the third finger of her left hand. It was no wonder she had knocked Jack senseless. She was a stunning beauty and seemed like a dear, sweet person as well.

"Oh.", Catherine replied as she quickly turned to go while hiding the tears that were beginning to well up in her eyes, "Not all of our admirer's are secret."

The lady stood and put a loving hand on Catherine's arm. It felt like a wisp of silk laying there.

"You okay, sugar?" she asked, "Do you know who our mysterious friend is?"

"I'm not sure", Catherine replied, her voice quivering.

"Well, I would like to thank him—I suppose it was man?" the lady purred.

"Yes, but you can't thank him. He doesn't work here anymore."

"Hmmm.", the lady was obviously running this information through her mind, "Well if you ever see him again, sugar, can you tell him how much I appreciate the songs?"

"Oh", Catherine replied, "I think he knows. He may have known more about us than we knew ourselves."

Before the lady could ask anything else, Catherine walked away.

There was nothing more she could say anyway. In his own endearing fashion, Jack had said it all.

THE END

RESURRECTION

The man tore at her jogging outfit.

Gina tried to resist, but his first blow had left her groggy and disoriented. The bastard! The cowardly bastard! If he would have tried to rape her straight on, he would have never laid a hand on her without getting severely damaged himself! Instead he leapt out of the shadows and struck her hard across her face before she had a chance to react.

She started to cry out; weren't rape victims told to yell "Fire" since people were more likely to respond to that call? But at her first sound, he put a stinking hand over her mouth. No telling where it had been. It was so dark, she couldn't see his face, couldn't identify him to the police if he let her live.

That thought made her struggle harder. But the combination of the five miles she had already run and his physical abuse left her weak.

Should she give in? Let him do what he wants, and then hopefully he will leave? No! This creature didn't want sex. She had always heard that rape was an act of violence towards women and not a sexual perversion. Most likely the man would try to hurt her some more even if she gave in.

Her jogging pants were now around her knees. She held them tightly together; he would have to fight for what he wanted.

He took his hand off her mouth and struck her hard again, then again, then once more. Now she was too tired and beaten to let out more than a whimper. Blood began to stream down her face. Sensing this he tore off her thin underwear. She could hear him unzipping his pants then felt his exposed body pressing on her, trying to make penetration.

Gina's strength was nearly gone, she had to relent and see what happened. Maybe he would just go away. After all, he had already beaten her up pretty bad.

Suddenly, the man was gone! What had happened? He hadn't just gotten up on his own; it was so sudden that it seemed as if he had been *lifted* off of her.

Through hazy eyes she looked up, a dim streak of light from a distant street lamp showed the man's face. He was saying something, apparently talking to someone, but she could see nothing in front of him except a darkened spot in the night.

"We was just havin' some fun, dude. No need to get sore. She's my girlfr—"

Before he could finish the lie, she heard a strange sound, like a cat suddenly frightened by a dog, she saw her attacker's head pitch forward into the darkness. The wind was being forcefully expelled from his body. Then there was a hard slapping sound along with that same odd cry. The man's head flew back into the glare of the street light. She could see that he was bleeding profusely. It looked as if his nose had been broken; his lips were split as well. He meekly put up his hands to defend himself, but the whirling spot of blackness in front of him, hit him along side the head with what looked like some type of black crooked club. The same peculiar cry accompanied the blow.

The man flew sideways and landed, hard, in the middle of the street. She could see him clearly now as he lay motionless.

She fell back in sheer exhaustion and confusion.

Soft padding steps came towards her. The black spot she had seen was now standing over her.

"Did he harm you, ma'am?"

The voice was that of a man. It was deep, resonant and very calming despite her situation.

"He hit me a couple of times, but I'll be okay. Who are you?"

"Just a friend ma'am. Get your clothes on and stay here until the police come. I will go call them now."

She could see nothing but the night talking to her. Still, she some how knew the man talking to her was looking at her eyes and not her exposed flesh.

"But . . ."

"Don't worry about him, ma'am. The only place he is going to is the hospital, then to jail for a long time."

"Will you at least tell me your name?"

The darkness seemed to hesitate; then it spoke, the deep voice cracking somewhat, as a black, glove covered hand, touched her softly on top of the head, "My name is nothing, ma'am since I am nothing. I exist only in the night, by day I am the walking dead."

He stopped short at that. He seemed to be thinking, his hand was still stroking her hair.

"Don't be afraid of the night ma'am. It can be a comforting cocoon for those who just wish to hide from the light. Remember that not all who dwell there are evil. If you prepare for the darkness, it will sustain you."

With that, the murky shape sprinted into the night.

She did as instructed.

*　　*　　*

Damn reporters! They were having fun at her expense again! The "Black Night", as some punster had dubbed him, had struck once more, this time saving an old man from being mugged while putting four armed hoodlums in the jail's hospital ward. So, yet again, the newspapers were erroneously crediting her with giving the man his nickname.

By the time the police arrived, apparently summoned by her rescuer as he had promised, she had recovered enough to get dressed. She was hurt, but not critically so. A policeman took her to the hospital in his patrol car; her assailant went in an ambulance. When she heard that he might not walk again, Gina thought that it was a pity he would live at all.

At the hospital she did her best to tell the officer what had happened. She could not give any description of the man who saved her, except to describe his voice and say he was wearing something that made him appear "Blacker than the night". A reporter, with too much time on his hands, must have gotten a hold of the statement and the next day it was headline news.

The cretin that had attacked her didn't help either. He kept telling anyone that would listen to him, especially reporters, that he was an innocent victim. He claimed that he was just walking along when he came upon Gina and a man having sex. The man got enraged at him for interrupting them and then proceeded to beat him up. He was unconscious after that and didn't know where the man had run off to, nor could he remember his face well enough to describe him.

The police locked him up until they could sort everything out.

Meanwhile the papers wrote what he said and what she said. Soon people began debating the "truth" while completely ignoring the facts that someone had beaten her badly and that her real boyfriend, Damon, proved that he was nowhere in the vicinity when she was attacked.

Now Damon was gone. Not only had he grown tired of having to vindicate himself to people who preferred an easy lie to the truth, he was beginning to wonder if Gina really had been with another man that night as her attacker was saying.

As mindless as this sounded, even to him, he could not get over his doubts.

He was angry with her and blamed her for the whole mess. In a moment of insanity, he went so far as to accuse of her running at night just so she *could* get raped. He acted as if she wanted to be humiliated and brutalized. He accused her of having a suppressed rape fantasy and this was a way to get what she wanted.

After that, she was glad he had gone. It took an ugly incident like this to show her what a pig he really was.

The rest of Gina's life was going to hell, too. She no longer ran at night; she no longer ran at all. The loneliness that accompanied long distance running was more than she could bear even in broad daylight and she wanted to be around people—as long as it was light enough to show their faces. Before darkness fell each night, she went home and locked herself in her apartment. She didn't answer the door and if anyone called they got her machine.

Soon, problems began to erupt at her work, too. There were the gossipers, the doubters, and the catty women who were jealous of her good looks. They felt just like her ex-boyfriend: she had wanted it but after luring a rapist to her, she was too afraid to go through with it. They whispered that she must have fought off her attacker then made up the whole "Black Night" tale. For these people, thinking was not an option when there was a good story on which to speculate.

Still, she could almost excuse people like them since they were the ones that always saw malevolence in everyone. The worse ones were the people who resented her forced "celebrity". After all, they said, it was only an attempted rape. Outside of a few cuts and bruises she was fine, so what was she whining about? How come her name was always in the paper, they asked?

Her boss, Mr. Marathe, was an older man who knew her well. He dismissed all of the gossip while comforting her as best he could. Anything she needed, time off for the doctor or police, help with avoiding prying reporters, assistance with the company's insurance people, anything at all, he was there to help. He had always treated her like a daughter and now she appreciated it more than ever.

But he could only do so much. She began to have fits of depression, which made her listless and caused her mind to wander. She couldn't sleep with the lights off and very little with them on. Every time she heard that her rescuer had saved another person, she fell deeper into depression as she longed for his touch. She wished that she could find the man and keep him to herself where he could always be besides her, protecting her, while telling her it was okay to go out into the night.

But no one could find him and as winter approached, the heavens and the Earth conspired to spin a cocoon of enveloping darkness that made the nights last longer. As it did, he became more active. There were times when he seemed to be everywhere at once. Each time he helped someone, a gaggle of reporters called her as if she could miraculously tell them who he was.

Suicide was beginning to sound like a good option to her—especially with the trial looming before her.

$*$ $*$ $*$

When they wheeled in the coward who had attacked her, Gina was nearly sick. Olivia, one of the Detectives assigned to her case, sat with her in court, patted her hand and whispered words of encouragement. She told her that with the evidence they had against her attacker, it would be short trial and there was no way that he would go free.

She was right, of course.

The Assistant District Attorney's DNA proof showed that the blood on the defendant's clothing belonged to Gina. There were also traces of skin from Gina's face on his knuckles.

Then there was the overworked, uncaring, public defender who represented the creep. He was a round faced, squat man, who performed his duties as if he had just graduated from law school a month ago. Though obviously young, he moved with a great deal of huffing and puffing as if the weight of the world were on his shoulders.

When the slimy little man cross-examined Gina about her past sex life, she felt violated all over again. She could tell that the jury did not like it either. Many of the people looked like they wanted to come out of the jury box and kick the man real hard.

Fortunately, though Gina enjoyed sex as much as any other healthy woman, she was neither promiscuous nor very experienced. In her 20 some years, she had only had two sex partners with Damon playing that role for the past 3 years. So, the questioning did not last long.

The only thing that was missing from the trial was the testimony of the Black Night who had saved her. Naturally, the newspapers were playing this up big.

In print they challenged him to come forward, to show himself, to prove that Gina did not just make him up. He never showed. Gina was glad because he would have, most likely, been arrested due to his activities. But she was sad because she frantically wanted to meet him.

However, the fact that she had been saved by him never came up in court. The Public Defender continued to, absurdly, contend that Gina had been having sex with "another man" when his client stumbled upon them and was then beaten by the man. Who the man was, they had no clue and no case.

It took the jury one hour to convict her attacker.

As Olivia walked Gina out of the courthouse, she told her that is was now time for her to get back to her life and put all this behind her.

Gina hoped that she would have the strength to do that.

*   *   *

It was the start of another miserable day. Gina reluctantly stumbled out of bed, went through the motions of bathing, brushing her teeth, combing her hair. None of it mattered, the pallor her skin had taken on made her look hideous no matter what. She knew it; she didn't care.

Fitting into her clothes was getting more difficult each day as well. Eating nothing but take out or delivery food was adding pounds to her small frame. This added weight made her look frumpy and disheveled all the time. She had thought about buying new clothes, be she had pretty much given up on shopping for anything. Lately she couldn't stand to go anywhere, day or night, where there were other people. She knew they were all looking at her and talking about her behind her back—she just knew it! So she avoided people. Her boss was kind enough to let her start working from home whenever possible, but some days she just had to go in and face her co-workers. Today was one of those days.

She picked up her car keys and hesitantly approached the door. First she looked out the peephole to see if anyone was waiting for her. All clear. Softly, so as to avoid any noise, she unhitched her chain lock, the dead bolt, and turned the doorknob. She threw it open while holding her keys like a weapon, ready to strike out at any hidden attackers. As she stepped out, her foot kicked something that went scuttling out in front of her. It was an envelope.

Picking it up, she saw her name neatly printed on it in clean block lettering. Probably something from one of those annoying reporters, she thought, even though she consciously knew they had pretty much been leaving her alone for that last few months.

Should she open it? Maybe her attacker had gotten out of jail and was after her now?

Going back into her apartment, she sat on her couch and slit the envelope open with her thumbnail.

There was a brochure in it for a local martial arts studio with the exotic name of Way of Orient. It was a rather plain looking production, obviously done at a cut-rate printer. Opening it, she read the usual sales pitch about why one should train to protect oneself, how martial arts prepare the body and mind for any type of daily activity, and more.

However, the person who left the information for her had taken the trouble to circle one particular offering from the school. Highlighted was a special class of self-defense for women.

This item made her mind race back to the night that had started her on her downward spiral. If she had been trained, would it have changed anything? Most likely not since her attacker took her by surprise. She felt like tearing the thing up, but something made her hesitate. She wasn't sure why, but something from that night and this brochure seemed to be connected. Realizing she would be late for work—again—she slipped the paper into her purse and ran out the door.

*   *   *

All day at work she thought about the pamphlet. Every now and then she would take it out and read it over. The school was not too far from her home but the class for women's self-defense was held at night. She couldn't take them.

Mr. Marathe saw her looking the information over and inquired about it so she let him read it. After seeing the part about the self-defense for women, he insisted she leave work immediately and go sign up for the class. She thanked him, but said she needed to think about it a little more, which she did for the rest of the day.

*   *   *

As Gina walked down the steps to the underground studio, a series of noises assaulted her ears. They were cries of the most unusual and assorted variety.

Peering in the window next to the studio door, she could see a line of students, dressed in loose fitting white, black, or red outfits. They were facing a large man who was leading them through a series of punching and kicking motions. With each motion, the students let out a yell.

After a few minutes, the instructor let the students stand at ease while commanding them to break up into groups to practice with each other. At his shouted command, they did as they were told.

Then he turned and looked directly at her. He motioned for her to come in. Hesitantly, she opened the door and entered.

"How did you like the drills?" the man asked, coming towards her, but not extending his hand.

When he stood in front of her, she realized that though the man was "big", he was not particularly tall, nor did he look the type to be taking a martial arts class much less teaching one. On the street, she would have thought of him as a construction worker. His hair was thinning, though he looked young, and his girth was more than some of the men in her office who she considered lazy.

He motioned her toward two large chairs located to one side of the doors.

"My name is Master Seventy, Kurt Seventy. What brings you to my studio?"

Suddenly a fracas broke out on the floor. Two students were fighting as the rest looked on. Master Seventy, not even turning his head to look, shouted something out in a foreign language. The fight stopped immediately. She must have looked very surprised.

"Things can get a little out of hand here as we try to learn with and from each other. The rule is that if you fight, full contact, without protective gear, you must fight me next. You may be surprised how little this happens."

He smiled and she felt instantly more comfortable.

"Now, how may I help you?"

Gina fished the brochure out of her purse and handed it to him.

"Did we send this to you?" he asked while looking it over, "This is one of our direct mail pieces."

"No. Someone gave it to me"

"Oh? A student of mine?"

"I don't know."

"You don't know if your friend is a student?"

"I don't know who it was. It was left on by my front door anonymously . . ."

Her face must have shown that this was disturbing to her in some way.

"However you came about this," he said soothingly, "I am glad you came in. Is there anything in particular that you are interested in?"

"I wanted to talk to you about the women's self-defense class. Are they only held at night?"

Master Seventy gave here a curious look, "Yes, I am afraid there is not enough of a demand that would warrant me teaching it more than once per week. I wish that were not the case. It is a very valuable class for women looking to defend themselves but not particularly interested in more intensive training."

"Oh. Well then thank you for your time," Gina replied as she stood to go.

"Please sit." Master Seventy said.

Though his tone was gentle, Gina felt the command in his voice. She sat back down.

"Can you tell me why you cannot attend the class at the stated time? Perhaps I can work something out for you?"

"It's held at night."

Master Seventy seemed not surprised by this response. He said nothing.

"I don't like going out at night." Gina whispered, embarrassed with herself, "I am afraid of the dark."

"I won't ask your reasons for this." Master Seventy replied, "That is not my affair. What is my concern is that we get you to where you are afraid no longer."

"How would we do that?"

He looked at her quietly for a moment. His eyes went up and down her body as if examining her for damages. She began to squirm a little under his intense gaze.

"You look fit. Perhaps you should take regular classes? I have two Saturday morning sessions where I let a younger teacher take over the class while I work individually with special students. Would you be interested in that?"

This would mean going out among people, Gina thought. But then it would only mean going here to this place where it seemed relatively safe with Master Seventy present and it would be in the daytime. Perhaps she should take a chance; it had been a long time now. She needed to break out of her self-imposed confinement and this seemed like a natural way to do it.

"How do I sign up?" she asked.

* * *

Gina's bones ached as she soaked in a hot bath. It had been a long time since she had taken part in any kind of physical activity much less the kind she had gone through the previous day. Now she could understand how one person could severely damage another person if they used the proper techniques. She felt like hell and the people at the school had been nice to her!

She had enjoyed being around other people in their fighting clothes or "ghis" as they called them. She blushed at the last thought. Having never worn one of these outfits, she didn't realize exactly how loose they were until Master Kurt (as the younger students referred to him) had softly thrown her during rolling drills. Next time she will be sure to where a t-shirt underneath it!

She smiled at how easily she thought about the "next time". This meant getting out of her apartment and being among people. For the first time in many months, she did not cringe at the idea as long as it meant being with the people at Way of Orient.

Getting dressed, she made a vow to get back into the kind of shape she had been in before her attack. She was determined to continue with the classes until she knew she could defend herself from any assault. Her inspiration came not from Master Kurt, though, it came from the kids in the class, especially the young girls, some as young as seven years old. She wondered what would have happened that night if she had been in training since such a young age. She smiled at the vision.

* * *

Saturday's could not come soon enough and before long the weeks of Gina's life that fell between them became meaningless. Her existence now revolved around her Tai Kwon Do lessons at Way or Orient. The strength and stamina, along with the nice figure she once had, were returning to her which each passing week. Her boss noticed the gradual change, and commended her on it, since she was now going into the office every day like all the other drones. Whether it was her newfound confidence in her step and stature or just the passing of time no one mentioned her near rape anymore.

Even her hero's actions didn't get that much of a mention anymore. He was still operating and still the law had not been able to take him into custody. Though, privately, she thought that they were not trying too hard anymore: the crime rate in town had been dropping steadily since he'd appeared. The only odd thing was that no one, besides her, had spoken to him. This made Gina feel special in a strange and curious way.

*   *   *

Master Kurt gaped in open wonder—for a few seconds—then he greeted Gina in the warm way he always did. It was Wednesday night when Gina had walked out of her apartment, gotten into her car, and then drove to the school for a class. He had never seen her out after dark since this was the first time since her attack she had ventured out without the Sun showing her the way.

Gina almost laughed at the surprise look on Master Kurt's face. Instead, she gave him a big bear hug since it was he who had finally set her free.

As she stepped back from him, she heard a sound that made her jump.

"Are you okay?" Master Kurt asked.

"That sound. What was it?"

Then she heard it again, this time repeated in rapid fashion.

Master Kurt stepped aside, nodding his head towards the far back corner of the room where a man was practicing alone. His hands and feet looked like blurred streaks as he punched and kicked at the air in front of him. The viciousness of his blows scared her as she thought about what was happening to his imaginary foe. The look on his cruel, yet oddly handsome, face was one of total concentration.

"That is his ki ai; you have heard "spirit shouts" before. You are developing a nice one yourself."

"But . . . but I have heard that one before."

"That is not possible, Gina. It must have been one that sounded similar. He only comes in on Wednesday night and this is your first evening visiting us."

"No, I have heard that one before; I have to talk to him."

As she made her way past, Master Kurt put a firm, but gentle hand on her.

"No. You must never talk to that man." It was a command.

"He practices here on special conditions. I honor his wishes, as it is a tribute to have him in my modest school. He only asks that he be left alone."

"I know who he is." Gina asserted.

At that Master Kurt assumed a look and stance she had never seen before. He seemed to rise up and tower over her. His voice was low, clear and commanding.

"No Gina. You do not know who he is."

He turned and walked away signaling the end of the discussion.

* * *

After that, Gina never missed a Wednesday night or a Saturday morning. Accordingly, her expertise rose rapidly. Soon she was making her way quickly through the belt ranks; she had even entered and won a school-sponsored tournament, which helped her advance more swiftly in rank. Finally she arrived at the Brown Belt level; the level Master Kurt called the "doorway to the upper ranks". She was thinking of stopping there, but after she thought about her long isolation—which seemed like a distant nightmare now—plus the time and effort she put into her studies, she decided to go on.

Fourteen, long, hard months later, she was ready to test for her Black Belt.

On the morning of the test, Gina could not sit still. She helped Master Kurt with testing of the lower belt ranks and ran errands as needed. Finally he pulled her aside.

"Gina, you need to slow down. The Black Belt test is five hours long. As you know, it is as much a test of stamina as it is skill. You need to save your energy."

"I will be fine, Master Kurt. I have so much adrenaline flowing now I could knock down brick walls."

"And what happens when the adrenaline runs out, Gina? Maybe in the middle of the test? Then what? No, you need to sit, now."

He pulled her to a corner chair and handed her a refreshing drink. As soon as she sat, she realized he had been right. She was fatigued more than she realized.

For the next two hours, she watched the testing. She always enjoyed seeing the young girls perform. They were often so limber and quick that they could throw amazingly fast and high kicks, some of which may have even rocked Master Kurt if they could connect.

Finally the Black Belt candidates were called to the testing area. The five of them, including Gina, were greeted with warm applause.

Master Kurt led the drills. During the kicking, punching, falling and seemingly endless forms drills, she never lost focus. She was so focused, that she did not see "him", as she came to think of her Wednesday night mystery man, come in. He was dressed in a new jet-black ghi. Over the months, she had wanted to approach him, but Master Kurt, apparently able to sense when she was weakening, would take her aside and admonish her.

Finally, in the fifth hour, came the fighting test where she had to take on four opponents at once. She was third up, so she was able to rest and watch as the other two candidates fought Master Kurt and three other Black Belts. They both acquitted themselves well. She was sure they would pass.

As she stood to approach the fighting floor, the crowd became very quiet. She thought it was because of the fact that she was the only female contestant. Consequently she was shocked when her mystery man stepped on to the floor to face off against her.

While bowing deeply towards him, Master Kurt, and two other students, Gina had a great urge to run out the door. Her knees were weak, and she felt a little dizzy. But there was no time for that, as soon as she straightened up, they were on her. This wasn't fair, she thought! The others had some time for introductions. Irrationally, she thought Master Kurt was making it especially hard on her because she was a woman. As illogical as that thought was, she was angry as she dodged and parried the kicks and punches of her attackers.

She had one great advantage over the other fighters, though. She was much lighter and thus very fast on her feet. Her runner's legs had also returned to her allowing her to dance on her toes without ever getting weary. As she swiftly danced around in alternating circles, she worked to line up her opponents in a row so she only faced one fighter at a time. The first person she met in this formation was Master Kurt.

She leapt, higher than she ever thought she could, and caught him with a flying sidekick to the chest—much to his surprise. This brought a thunderous round of applause from the crowd. As she landed, she danced between the other two students while they still were dazzled by her leap. She punched the one in front of her three times then launched a back sidekick at the one behind her that sent him flying. Before she could turn her attention back to "him", she felt a thump on the side of her head. The blow made her lose her balance sending her to the floor. In anticipation of the next attack, she flipped to her back and kicked blindly up at the oncoming figure, sending it sprawling to the floor on its backside.

She quickly stood in readiness for the next attack, which did not come.

If possible, the hush on that came over the crowd was even quieter than before. Sitting on the floor before her was her mystery man. She bowed to her opponents. The crowd erupted.

Master Kurt came forward and shook her hand. Her test was over.

*   *   *

"I know who you are."

He turned, almost as if he had been expecting her.

"I know that, Gina. I'm sure you have known for a long time."

"How do you know my name? Master Kurt would never let me talk to you."

"I saw it in the paper—many times—not that long ago . . ."

The memories of those days came flooding back to Gina like a nightmare scenario. She had all but forgotten those times. They seemed to be in a past life remembered.

"Why?" she had to know.

After all this time, it was her only question for him.

"It was an accident really, Gina. I didn't go out on that night looking to save anyone. I had just been prowling the streets in my Ninja gear as I had been doing since—since a time past. Seeing the situation you were in, though, I couldn't let it continue. Afterward, I felt so good about what I did, I did it again. Now, I will continue to do it until it is stops feeling good."

"Or until you're killed!" she stepped forward and hugged him tight.

His hand went up to the top of her head and stroked her hair as he had done the first night they had met. His touch was soft and gentle. Gina buried her face even deeper in his chest. She was crying profusely, her tears soaking the front of his ghi. She loved him desperately.

"If I am, it is of no consequence, Gina. As I told you once, I only exist in the night, by day I am the walking dead."

Gina looked up at him, "Why do you say that? What makes you to say such a thing? You are so alive in my eyes."

"But I am not Gina. I am only alive on the outside. What you see is a shell, an empty shell . . ."

"No! You're not. I can feel your heart beating, I can hear you breathing, and I can see the intelligence in your eyes. You are more alive than any man I have ever met and you saved me, not once, but twice."

He gazed knowingly at her.

"I thought you had figured that out."

"Yes, after I saw you here and realized who you are, I knew that you were the one who left the school's brochure at my door step. How did you know?"

"I had been watching you. I wanted to make sure you were all right. When I realized what was happening with you—not leaving your apartment after dark or going to work—I knew I had saved your sweet body only. You mind now needed to be rescued."

When he mentioned her body, she snuggled it up closer to him. She felt him react to it. Now it was he who needed saving.

"And you did. More than that, you improved me. You lead me to a path where, if I worked hard enough, I could redeem myself. I have never felt so alive. You must stay with me now. You must stop saying you're dead, yet alive. I love you so much."

She felt his strong body relax somewhat. His lips came down on top of her head and kissed it softly. He began to cry.

"What happened to you to make you feel that way? It must have been something terrible."

"My wife—"

He was married?

"My wife was killed by a rapist."

Gina's mind reeled. What kinds of forces were in play here? Was she and this man just a pair of puppets whose strings were being manipulated by the erratic hands of fate? She held him tighter.

"I couldn't save her the way I saved you. I wasn't at home when the man forced his way into our house then raped and murdered her. So when I saw you with that beast on top of you, I felt that I had been given a second chance in some way."

"Yes!" Gina cried out, "You have been given a second chance. Just as I've been given another chance. That's why you have to go on living. You have to stop taking these wild chances."

"You have to know I can't stop, Gina. Not even for you. I won't stop until I have expended all of my hate towards the kind of man that killed my wife, the kind of man that will prey upon only the weak. I am showing them all what it is like to be on the other side."

Gina understood this. She had wanted to go out and kill a rapist, robber, or murderer—any criminal—after she had been attacked.

Still, she loved him so.

"They'll never learn. You can stop as many as you dare in your lifetime, but you won't stop them all since they will keep coming as long a man survives on this planet. These people are acting on a function of what we are and were animals, all of us. Yes we have higher thought processes, we can build a world of wood and steel, we can make love, create war, go to other planets, we can do all these things, but we can never stop being what we are. We are animals no more, no less, no matter how you dress it up."

"Would you really have me stop, Gina?"

Yes, she thought!

"No. I mean, I don't know. I understand, I really do, but I don't want to lose you. I don't know what to do."

"Then let's not make any decisions now, Gina. Let's go home and talk more about it. Then we can decide when our minds are clearer."

"Yes", she replied, "let go home . . . to your home?"

"Yes, Gina, for tonight, my home."

She kissed him passionately.

"Okay, your place tonight, my place tomorrow night . . ."

*   *   *

Kurt slowly shook his head as he read the morning paper. It looks like he would have to talk to his prize students again on Wednesday night. He had to show them that they were playing the wrong game. That someday they may regret it more than they now realize. Still, there were nights when he had a great urge to join them . . .

*   *   *

The Ventura Valley Times

On the Internet: *www.tvvt.com*   Saturday, March 19, 2005   Copyright 2005 / 97 pages   35 cents

The Black Night Takes a Mate?

Confirming earlier rumors, the so-called Black Night vigilante appears to have taken a mate.

Last night, on opposite sides of town, two attacks on law-abiding citizens were thwarted within mere minutes of each other consequently confirming that there are now two denizens of the night menacing nocturnally inclined criminals.

The perpetrator on the east side claims to have struck his attacker and swore that he heard a woman cry out. The two teenage girls that he was assaulting confirmed his story. Police plan further interrogation of the man once his condition is stabilized.

Gina Hendricks, who was the first person to benefit from the original vigilante's actions, was not available for comment before we went to press.
(See Black Night, Page A28)

THE END

BUDDHA'S DREAM

Part One: *RADIO TALK*

"Hey man, what's up?"

"Not much buddy, same old crap just a different day. You know how it is."

"Yeah man, I do. Hey, did you catch Jim Lloyd on the radio last night?"

"Naw. The old lady was raggin' on me about how much I been drinkin' lately, so I got pissed off and went out for a few beers. Man, she's gettin' to be a real pain. You know how it is."

"Yeah, I do. Anyway, you missed a damn good show, man. Our homeboy Jimmy was really cooking. He got himself into some real heavy dream tripping schemes. Made me want to go to sleep forever. You ever feel like that?"

"Every friggin day, buddy. Every friggin day."

"Me too. Sometimes anyway."

"So what was his basic line, buddy? What'd he say about dreams?"

"Well man, he played a bunch of tunes about dreams and the people dreaming them. They went on an on, all about the same thing. When he was done he had people call in and try to guess why he played all these songs. He wanted them to figure out how all of them fit together. He wanted people to tell him what was in his mind. Man it was getting heavy."

"Sounds like it."

"Yeah, so anyway this dude calls in and says that he thinks that Jimmy boy is saying that maybe this world we live in is just someone's dream. Maybe this stuff that we think is real is just something that someone's is dreaming about. Well Jimmy just about flips out. He says 'Lord have mercy. You got it right on the first try. I tell you I've got the most intelligent listeners in radio.' or something like that."

"The hell you say? Sounds like our boy was wired."

"No man, he don't do that crap. This was just some heavy rap he's laying down."

"Maybe so. What else did he say?"

"Well first he gives this guy some great tickets to see someone; I think it was ZZ Top, or someone. Anyway it was a great pair of ticket's man, wish I'd a got them. But I didn't have no idea what he was putting out."

"You can't hardly get through to that boy anyway. It's just luck if you do."

"Yeah, you got that right. Anyway, he goes on and asked this dude if he ever heard about some religion that believes that their god is just sleeping and dreaming about all this around us. He thinks it is Buddhism, but he ain't sure."

"Was it?"

"Hell if I know. The dude on the radio didn't know if this was true or not either. He was clueless."

"He must have just been guessin' about the first stuff."

"Yeah, a good guess I guess. Anyway, I been thinking about all this ever since last night. No matter what Jimmy boy played after that, I couldn't get out of the mood that he put me in. Even after he went off the air and I was playing some of my own stuff, I couldn't get his question out of my head. What if all this was just a dream. Then what?"

"Then what what? Who cares, buddy? If this is all just a friggin' dream, we got to live in it no matter what. It's all a couple of dumb bastards like you and I got."

"Yeah man, but if all this is just a dream of some super person, then all this ain't nothing but a pile of crap. Our whole lives are nothing but crap. No matter what we think we do with our lives, we ain't doing nothing. This sucker could wake up any minute and all we got will be gone."

"Well we don't got much so it isn't ain't no great loss."

"Yeah but what we got, we got. I don't like thinking that someone else is making this all up because he ate something the night before that gave him indigestion. I like to think I got some control."

"Well you don't have any, buddy. None of us has got none. There isn't anyone in this whole friggin' world that don't have someone controllin' them, and I don't give a damn what anyone thinks about that. Even if there is a guy dreamin' us, he has got to get up sometime and when he does he'll have an old lady raggin' at him and a boss who wants him to kiss his ass. He'll be just like us."

"Yeah, you may be right. But when he gets up, we will all be gone. All that we got will be lost."

"Look buddy, you are talkin' like this 'that we got' is something special. Well it isn't. Anyway, if this is all a dream than we can just go out and do what ever it is that we want. Right? Well isn't that right? If this is all a dream and don't mean nothin' than we can do what we want today since tomorrow night this guy might go back to sleep and dream us another way. Hell, I might be someone important and not just some dumb loser who don't have a pot to piss in or a window to throw it out of."

"Yeah but what if it isn't a dream. What if Jimmy boy was just goin' off like he does sometime? Then what?"

"Then nothing. True reality or made up reality. Someday were all goin' to go 'poof' weather it happens cause some guy wakes up or if it happens when you get hit by a beer truck. We all got to go 'poof' someday. So all this now don't mean diddley."

"Yeah man, you may be right. But it's tough to think about it sometimes."

"Then don't think, buddy. Just do it. And do it quick cause the man controllin' us may wake up anytime."

* * *

Part Two: NIGHT TALK

"What?? What the hell? Who's there? Stop! I gotta gun man and I'll use it."

"You don't got no gun, buddy. Ever since we was kids, you never liked them. So don't bullshit me."

"Man! What the hell you doing sneaking in here in the middle of the night like this? How the hell did you get in anyway??"

"I came through the window in the front room, the one with the broken lock. Remember, I was the one that broke it when we were throwin' things around during that football game last year. You never did fix it."

"Yeah man, I remember; but what're you doing here? Where's your old lady. Does she know your here? She's going to be mad as hell."

"I'm hidin' buddy. And my old lady don't know I'm here and she don't care no more either. I killed her."

"What'd you say? You're just putting me on aren't you?"

"It's true, buddy. I killed her. She's dead."

"But why, man? Why?"

"'Cause she kept raggin' and raggin' and raggin' at me, buddy. Tonight it was worse than ever. She said I was stupid, that my job didn't pay crap and that she was sorry she didn't marry a real man instead of me."

"Oh man she was always saying that and you never killed her before."

"I know, but tonight I tried to tell her not to worry so much. I tried to tell her about the stuff we was talkin' about tonight. I tried to tell her that this here life was nothin' but a dream of some guy sleepin' on a cosmic couch somewhere. I wanted her to know that if things were bad tonight, in this dream, things were bound to be better tomorrow in the next one. Tomorrow she might be a queen and I might be her king. Then she would be proud of me. I also told her I loved her now whether she was a queen or an street walker, like she used to be."

"What did she say to that, man?"

"She laughed! She laughed and she kept on laughin'! She said that my boozin' had finally turned my brain to slush. Then she asked why I thought she wasn't walkin' the streets no more. She asked me what I thought she was doin' all the nights while I was out boozin' and messin' around with you; stayin' home like a lovin' wife? Like hell! She said she was out doin' it again and she was likin' it. A lot! Said it was a pleasure to be with a real man again after livin' with me. Then she laughed some more. That's when I done it. That's when I killed her an' all the time I was doin' it I was tryin' to tell her that I was doin' it for her. The way she looked at me, I knew she hated me, but you gotta understand I was savin' her buddy. I loved her. I could never give her anythin' in life, so I wanted to give her somethin' in death. I took her out of this dream an' put her in another one that I know has to be a better one than this."

"Oh man, oh man, oh man! You tore it this time, you know that? You really tore it."

"I know, buddy. That's why I'm hidin'. She screamed plenty before I could shut her up. I just know someone called the cops. I know they're lookin' for me."

"Yeah, and the first place they will look is here. Everyone knows I'm your best buddy."

"You're my only buddy. Your the one that finally set me straight on how things were in this world. I know that I laughed at you tonight, but the more I thought about it the more I knew that you were right."

"What do you mean I was right? I wasn't nothing! All that talk was just talk, man. Radio talk. The kind of stuff people talk about all the time. I don't believe it."

"It was more than that, buddy. You may not believe it, but what you said was right. Jimmy boy was right. You was both right. This here reality is all a dream. We can change it anyway we like right now because tomorrow night it will be all different anyway. None of this here around us means anything to anyone. My old lady is okay right now, buddy. I saved her. You got to believe me about this. Sure I killed her in this reality, so now she isn't a part of this dream. Tomorrow night she will be alive again, she will have things better. You will see, buddy. She will be all right. She may have hated me while I was killin' her, but she knows now that I saved her life. I was her cosmic savior. By doin' what I did, I gave her a better life."

"I don't know, man. I mean that's okay if that's what you believe. But now she is dead; she isn't all right. What's to become of you now? Your still awake."

*   *   *

Part Three: END TALK

"Hey man, how you doing? They treating you okay."

"Sure buddy! Theys treatin' me like I only got a few more days to live! Now isn't that a crack up. I've been treated like garbage all my life. Now that theys gettin' ready to kill me, suddenly I'm a bundle of roses; they can't do enough for me. I guess theys all doin' this cause theys glad it ain't them goin' to the big sleep."

"Now don't say that man. I been talking to your lawyer and he says that they might let you off. He says that another judge just might believe you were crazy when you killed your old lady. You just got to stop pretending like you believe all that crap you been telling them."

"You don't get it buddy. Ever since you told me all that stuff about dreams and reality, I've been believin' it. I believe it now."

"Oh man, you don't mean it."

"But I do. I do. They thought I was fakin' it so I would get off as a loony, but I wasn't tellin' no lies. Even you told them that I thought what I was sayin' was true."

"You got to forgive me, man. Those lawyers got me completely twisted up while I was talking in front of all those people. I didn't know what I was saying. They made me look like a fool. I am a fool."

"You're no fool buddy. And I don't forgive you cause you didn't do nothin' except tell the truth. They just chose not to believe us. They thought I wanted to be free. They didn't know that the moment I killed my old lady I was free."

"What are you saying now, man? More loony talk?"

"No. No loony talk. They might think it's loony talk, but it isn't. Not to me it isn't. And it never will be. You see buddy, the moment before I killed the old lady, I became convinced that I was right about this dream thing. If I hadn't been, I would never have had the nerve to kill her even though I thought about it often enough before I did it. By killin' her I knew that nothin' I did here and now meant nothin'. I knew then that for the first time in my whole stinkin' life, I was in command. I was in command even if I was just bein' dreamed by some fat slob lyin' in his bed."

"Stop man, no more of this crap, please."

"But it ain't crap buddy! It's true, you got to believe me. They may kill me, but you got to go on livin' so you got to believe, buddy. It's the only way your ever goin' to be free."

"So what do you want me to do? Go kill someone?"

"No buddy. That was my part of the dream. That was what I had to do to be free. I've had a lot of time to think while I been in my cell and the way I figure it, we all got somethin' that will trigger our freedom. We just got to find what that trigger is and pull it. It ain't right takin' someone else's life like I did, but that was the trigger I needed and I only did it 'cause I know that I just put the old lady to sleep. Right now she is waitin' to be dreamed by someone else and when that someone else goes to sleep, she will live again. This time things will be better for her; she won't have to marry a worthless bum like me."

"I don't know man . . . maybe. But I tell you, I'm gonna miss you when you go. We been buddies ever since we were kids and I love you man."

"And I love you to buddy. Your the best buddy any man could have, but don't worry, it will all be okay."

"You sure buddy?"

"Man I know it will be."

"But theys goin' to kill you."

"They're not going to kill me, man. They just think they are. You see, they think that by killing me everything will be okay again but it won't change anything, they have no control. Only the guy on the couch has control and I figure that, hey, I may be that guy. Now I think some of them believe me too! The guards who watch me everyday, the doctor who comes to see me most days, they all are starting to believe me. They protest and say they doubt me, but I see the fear in their eyes when they are denying me. They are afraid of going poof the second I wake up.

Even when they tell me about how they are going to do it I here them talking just like me. They say they are going to give me a 'lethal injection'. They say it will be painless; just like going to sleep. Isn't that the limit? They are saying death is like going to sleep, just like I've been saying all along. And it is true. Man, I am going to sleep just as this guy is waking up. That's why I think he and I are the same guy. Were just two halves that make up the whole of our being. He can't live without me and I can't live without him. When he goes to sleep, I live in his dream. When I sleep, he lives in mine. It's an endless circle."

"But what if you're wrong buddy? What if you're wrong?"

"I don't think I am wrong and even if you doubt me, it could work that way couldn't it?"

"I don't know, buddy. I just don't know. I've always been too dumb to remember my own name half the time, how could I decide on something like this? How could anyone know?"

"There's only one way man; I just got to go to sleep to find out."

THE END

HEROISM

MYRON? THE HERO?

"I will endeavor to do my best, to explain to you, officer, all the events that, um, er, have occurred in the past few hours. It all started with a knock on my door when, in a fit of foolishness, I decided to answer this summons. I don't do this often because I never know who will be there. It could be a con-man, a beggar, or worse yet, a salesperson! I am always telling my friend at work, Joe Budinzky, that I never answer the door because of the horrors that could lurk there. You know, I am not sure if he believes me. He just sort of sits there in the lunch room grunting and making off hand comments about this or that. I am not sure if he even listens to me as his responses are not always that cogent. I guess you could say that he is not even my friend, but he is the only one who will sit with me at lunch! Come to think of it, I am the only one who will sit with him—no matter how he smells. We just sort of paired off by Hobsons' choice, if you know what I mean."

"Oh? Your right officer, I am digressing in my narration."

"What? Yes, officer, I do tend to ramble."

"To continue, let me say that I was feeling very chipper today after Patty, the pretty girl who works in the mail room smiled at me. What a thrill!"

"Anyway, she smiled in my direction. That counts doesn't it officer? Doesn't it?"

"But this is the point officer. I would never have answered the door if it had not been for this overwhelming sense of accomplishment that had followed me home tonight. I was cocky and confident, so I strode to the door in full regalia! Of course this is what started my adventure!"

"For there on my door step was a shaggy, dirty, unshaven man in faded and torn blue jeans. He wore an overcoat that was much too heavy for the current weather. Underneath it I could see that he was wearing nothing but a tattered T-shirt. He was a sight!"

"But beyond all these trappings, officer, the most telling feature of the man were his hands which he kept tucked in his front pants pockets. You see, even though he tried to keep them out of sight, my fine eye for detail—I do have one you know—caught something very odd. Very odd indeed!"

"I could make out a letter tattooed on each index finger just above the knuckle!"

"On one finger of his left hand I could see a 'T' and on the right hand I could see an 'M'. These letters are what prompted me to examine his anatomy further. In doing so, I observed that the bulge in his left pocket was just slightly smaller than the bulge in his right one. This made a shiver run down my back like I had never felt before! It was as if the cold hand of death had patted me on the back!"

"My close scrutinization of him and my ensuing discomfort seemed to put him off a bit, but he still had the gall to ask me if I needed any work done around the house in exchange for a meal. Of course I told him that I did not need anything done, that I did everything for myself, thank you! Not only is this true, officer, but it gave me an excuse to slam the door right in his evil looking face!"

"Even though I was too shaken to look, I could tell that he did not immediately leave my premises. You see, my extra sharp hearing, just like my mother had, that sort of thing his hereditary, you know, did not detect any tell-tale retreating foot steps. I heard the man just sort of shuffling around on the porch as if he were in a state of indecision. Was he once more going to try to win my confidence or was he just going to leave? With a loud click, I threw the dead-bolt on my door. This seemed to have made up his mind as he left almost without delay."

"For a moment officer, I thought I was going to be violently ill. My internal organs shook so bad that I just had to collapse in a ball on the spot. I just had to!"

"Somehow I managed to climb into my recliner over there and slowly got my knees to stop from shaking while my senses came to some sort of order. And do you know why I was so frightened, officer? Do you?"

"Oh your right. You don't. That is why I am telling the story and not you."

"Anyway, officer, I was terrified so because *I knew that man*! Not personally, of course. I mean, before that very moment, I never laid eyes on him in the flesh. But I knew him. I had seen him on one of my TV shows!"

"You heard me right, officer. On one of my TV shows. You see, I like to watch all of those 'reality' shows that are on the airwaves now and my favorite one is the one where they exhibit pictures and stories of wanted criminals so people can see if they are associated with such low-life characters. If they are, they can call the show. Then the people at the show will dispatch the proper authorities and have the scoundrel rounded up."

"Do you ever watch that show, officer?"

"No? Oh, your job keep you much to busy to watch it? Too bad. Do you have a VCR? I do. That way I can keep track of all these good shows even when I am not here. What? Okay, okay, don't get mad, I will get back to the story."

"At any rate, this guy, who a moment before was standing on my doorstep, was one of those low-lifes! How did I know? I told you that I had a good eye for detail—I have, you know—well I also have a very good memory—something else I inherited from my mother!—well, even though this guy looked seedier than he had been on the TV show, I thought I recognized his face. But it was his hands, what little of them I saw, that made me so certain of his identity."

"The man that I suspected him to be had two words tattooed on his fingers just above the knuckle. On his left hand, he had the word "too" and on his right hand he had the word 'much'—'Too much'! The host on that new show, *Really Bad People*, said that this person, who I thought the stranger was, had these tattoos put on as a "macho thing". You see, as a child, the suspect had his left pinkie cut off accidentally while he and his dad were chopping wood. After that day, all the other kids teased him about not having enough fingers to do some of the things they did. This constant teasing battered the man's self-esteem so much, that he became angry and spiteful towards the world. I understand this part of the man's psychology, officer. As a child, I was teased a lot, too. I guess we all just react to things differently. I grew up timid and shy while he grew up mean and nasty. Because of his attitude, he brawled a great deal. This not only got him into trouble with the law, it also made him become known as an excellent street fighter. So, he always told people that even though his hands were inadequate in one way; they were 'too much' for most people. Thus the tattoos."

"Now the man is wanted for a murder committed during one of these street fights. And what happens? Here that violent character shows up on my very doorstep, staring me in the face, while on the run from the law!"

"All these thoughts about this man were swirling around in my mind as my biological functions had time to restore themselves. Once my legs were working again I did what I knew I had to do. I went to my telephone and called the TV show."

"Why yes officer, I do keep the number handy."

"But it was not until I called them that I realized that they only take calls for a short time before, during, and after the show. The recorded message told me to call the local police. This I did."

"No need to thank me, officer. You were the next logical choice. I just wish you would have come sooner. That way you would have not arrested the wrong man!"

"Yes, I know now that it was a mistake officer, but how did you think I felt being manhandled like that? Being locked up in the back or that patrol car with those awful handcuffs on was degrading."

"Of course I knew that I was almost incoherent on the phone when I called in, but I was so afraid that I thought I would be ill. The dispatcher should have known that something was terribly amiss just from the shaking in my voice."

"Yes I know that these people get a lot of crank calls, but I doubt that anyone could fake being as afraid as I was at that very moment. I was frightened! Right down to my bones! But I felt that I had to do something, I could not just sit back while this dangerous man wandered around my neighborhood. There are a lot of kindly old folks around here who would readily let a man like that in for the offer of him doing a chore for them in exchange for a meal. That is why I followed him when your dispatcher refused to send immediate help."

"At first I thought that I may have been too long in recovering from my initial trepidation, because when I did get up the courage to go out, I saw not a trace of him."

"Well let me tell you officer, I panicked again. I could feel the blood running draining from my face as I ran around the neighborhood searching for him. I was awash in self disgrace, officer. If this criminal hurt someone, the blood of this deed would be on my hands for I knew who he was and I did not, at first, act rationally enough to apprehend him."

"Illogical or not, officer, that is how I felt and it was a good thing for Mrs. Baker that I did; my guilt managed to overpower my cowardice and drove me to action. When I finally caught up with that man two blocks over and one down from here, he was just entering her house. Officer, Mrs. Baker was a life-long friend of my mother. When mom died, Mrs. Baker came by or called me daily for months afterward just to see if I was getting along all right. In a way, she took my mother's place, yet when I saw this man-monster enter her house, I still could not at once react. Instead I stood behind a tree feeling deathly ill."

"What was I to do officer? I had called you people but if you were coming, you were going to my house three blocks away! What was I to do? Take a chance that you would pass by? Go back to my house and wait for you to show up? Or do I act like a man?"

"Officer, for the first time in my life I did the latter. I arose from my sickness, ran to Mrs. Baker's door and pounded on it while calling for her. I suppose I expected some type of immediate response, but when none came, I tried the door only to find it locked fast. I became terribly distraught; where was Mrs. Baker? The man had only entered the house a few minutes before, had he already killed her? What had become of Mrs. Baker?"

"It was these thoughts that propelled me into the action that I was undertaking when you arrested me."

"As you recall, I was running around the house shouting at the top of my lungs, beating on all the windows and doors. I realize now that all of this caterwauling was mostly unintelligible noise, but it may be that this was a blessing in disguise. For as far as I can figure out, from what you told me, my very first outburst scared the murderer out the back door while terrifying Mrs. Baker so much that she would not answer my calls—even if they had made any sense! Fortunately I was loud enough so that the neighbors called you to the scene. That's when you roughed me up."

"No need to apologize, ma'am. I suppose I would have done the same thing in the light of the situation. Besides, you had the presence of mind to understand what was making me act so and you were able to decipher enough out of the chaos to call for more help. It was one of your back up units—I love police talk!—that apprehended the fleeing criminal."

"Now. Do you have a full understanding of the situation?"

"Good. Am I now free to go on with my life as it was?"

"No? Me, a hero? I don't think I can lay claim to that title—at least not directly. But I must admit that I am anxious to tell Joe Budinzky about all of this tomorrow at lunch. Maybe even the word will get around to Patty in the mail room; she might even smile at me for real. And officer, that would be nice!"

THE END

RUNNING MAN

His lungs heaved in his chest. His heart pounded so fast that it would surely burst if he kept up this pace. His old legs felt as if they would come apart at the knees at any moment. But still he ran.

He had to reach his destination.

Things just could not turn out again as they had all those many years ago.

He knew that this thought is what drove him on now. But then that is what drove everyone isn't it?. The memories of the past creating the future? As he ran, he wondered where the first "past" came from—what started the world turning? Not that it mattered now; his past was over, his future, if he would have any, and that of the youth, depended on the next few moments. He had to reach his target!

He wondered if it would be this way now if it had not been for Douglas then? Would he be running as fast? Would he be inviting his own end if it had not been for young Douglas? He was not sure. He had always been a judicious man, always looking for "right"—the meaning of the word etched and honed in his mind by seven decades of a hard, cruel life. Still after all these years he could not say exactly what it meant to be right. Had he ever been right? Was he right now? Would only time tell?

He was closing fast. As fast as he could anyway. While fighting for each breath, he remembered what it was like when he was younger. Then, even as little as twenty years ago, it would not be a race against life and death. He would have already been there. The moment would be over. But now, it was different. The numerous steps he had lost in two decades may prove to be too much to overcome.

Still he was making better time than most men his age could do. As a young man, he had been exemplary in track and swimming, it was this conditioning that aided him now even at what he felt was a plodding pace.

As his body worked on his mind realized that the last part would be the most difficult, he knew that his jump would have to be perfect, the push just enough to do the job. If the youth bumped his head, if he scraped a knee, so what? The alternative would be too horrible to think about. His mind, as an organized mind would do, began to calculate the mathematics of the move. A hopeless gesture from someone who was never particularly good with numbers, but the thoughts kept his mind preoccupied so it could not dwell on the pain now racking his body.

Words that meant nothing to him flew in his head: algorithms, trajectories, inertia, etc. All just words perceived in a lifetime of hearing, all meaningless, but words that, he knew, had to do with what may be final act of his life. Words that would mean little in the end except for the fact that they gave him something to do.

A few more labored strides and he was there! Then disaster struck. The curb was higher than the thought, the step down far greater than he imagined. He stumbled, caught himself, and lunged! Both feet made good purchase with the pavement and he was flying, flying! Just like a bird, just like the super hero's he had read about as child so long ago. And like these heroes, he was coming to the rescue!

As his hands reached to push the youth out of the way of the car that was now going to take his life instead, he was happy that, unlike those super heroes, he was not indestructible. For now he would be free. Free to go see Douglas, his own child that he had not been able save from the path of a speeding car so many decades ago. Now he would be free, free of the guilt, free of the shame he had always felt. Free, free, free!!!

As the car struck him, he saw that the child was safe, and again he was flying, flying, flying . . . .

* * *

"Calm down lady, calm down."

"But officer, is he dead? I didn't see him. He came flying out of nowhere, you must believe me! I didn't mean to hit him."

"I'm sure you didn't lady, but that doesn't change a whole lot."

"What do you mean, officer."

"Well you see that other lady over there hugging that kid?"

"Yes, officer, why is she crying?"

"I imagine she's crying because she is happy"

"Happy! How could she be happy at a time like this?"

"She's happy because according to the witnesses, you hit that old street person lying dead over there instead of her kid. Now do you get it?"

"That is why he came running in front of my car? The old fool. He must be a crazed alcoholic or something."

"You can stop talking that crap, lady. I knew that old boy. Sure, he lived on the streets; he has done so most of his life since his son was killed, years ago, by a speeder like you. But he was a decent man; he never drank or caused trouble. He just wanted to be left alone, he didn't want any part of society."

"Like I said officer, he sounds like a lunatic. No wonder he jumped in front of my car."

"And like I said, lady. Stop talking bad about the old man. Now!"

"But, but . . . ."

"Can it lady, I'm not in the mood!"

"I'm going to report you for this rude treatment officer!"

"Well, that's just fine with me lady, because like I said, the fact that you killed an old man instead of a young child doesn't change anything. You can tell my superior about my behavior down at the station. You're under arrest."

"But, I didn't mean to . . . ."

"Come with me."

THE END

HAIRY HERO

Hero stood up and stretched. On a hot day like today, Hero knew exactly why the Verticals called this time of year the "dog days" even though he himself was of the felinus family. When it was this hot and you had a full coat of hair, life could be rather miserable. Hero could just never figure out how the Verticals knew of such things.

For these Verticals were far from the most intelligent or rational life forms that he had come across in his long existence. Though the had lived with some of them in the past, Hero had no urge to do so again. He had found that their quirks and eccentricities outweighed only their vast ignorance of other life forms. Their belief that other animals were less intelligent than they were was easily the most irritating aspect of their being.

Why the Verticals did not even have enough stored collective memory to understand what level of existence they occupied in their lifeplain! They were easily the most deficient of life forms in collective memory. When compared to Hero's family group, Verticals had been around less time than the wink of eye!

But so much for that! It was now mid-morning and Hairy had still not bothered to find something to eat; he never did like scrounging when the temperature reached this level, but the gnawing in his stomach insisted that it be put to rest, so Hero grudgingly arose and went out in hopes of finding a quick, easy meal.

The abandon mobile unit that had been his resting place for the night turned out to be more than satisfactory for Hero. He made a mental note of its location and vowed to return to it if his paths ever lead this way again. The Verticals habitats that were in the same neighborhood were just as abandoned and dilapidated as the old mobile unit, so Hero knew that he would not get any hand outs from local tenants if he did come across any. More than likely he would have to avoid them so as not to turn into a meal himself. What an unpleasant thought!

Hero realized that one day he would have to ascend to the next existence level, but he wanted to be the one to pick the time and mode of travel to this place. At his advanced age, Hero favored passing through The Portal in his sleep.

Making his way down the dusty streets while watching out for functioning mobile units, Hero kept his sharp eyes on the look out for movement of a subspecies that he had heard frequently during the night.

At times their squeals had been so close to Hero that he realized they had not detected his presence. These animals, that the Verticals called "rats", (he could only assume that they did not know their proper name), normally kept a great distance between themselves and Hero's species because some of his kind liked to devour them at every opportunity. Hero was not this way. He never liked the tastes of these rats. He only ate them to satisfy his hunger and when he needed the mental lift that came by inheriting his victims stored memory; these rats had a wealth of remembrance having been in existence for great many eons. Every time Hero ate one of them, he felt more kin to their feelings and troubles.

In many ways they had the same type of social organization problems that Verticals have but, to their credit, they were free of the emotional deviations of that larger animal. One time Hero tried to communicate his feelings to a group of rats, but because of the animosity caused by past generations (something the Verticals called prejudice) between his type and theirs, they scurried off before he could finish his dissertation to them. The crazy language barrier had not helped either.

Although he prided himself on being a linguist, "rat" was one language he had not mastered. This was not so much a matter of intellect as it was a matter of physical differences. Hero could understand most of what they said, but because of the limitations of his vocal cords he could not mimic them. The little animals also had a sophisticated pattern of speech where one sound could be said exactly the same way with a different tone thus making each have separate meanings. And with their caste system the way it is, a lower animal could say the same thing as a higher one yet each animal would be saying something different. This was a totally confusing aspect to Hero since all these rats looked alike to him!

A noise in the distance caused Hero to prick up his ears! Was that a squeal of one of his quarry? Standing motionless, Hero listened. Yes! Off in a distance he heard the sound again! It was definitely "rat," but he could not make out the word that was spoken, although the intent seemed clear, the squeal was a signal to others of its kind to come to the area. Hero knew he had to move quickly now! In small groups, these rats became easily intimidated, but in a pack they became fearless warriors!

Using the stealth that he had inherited from his long dead ancestors, Hero moved slowly in shadows cast by the bright sunlight. His acute sense of smell had now caught the scent of the lesser animals. They were converging on the area he was approaching with a sense of speed that he had rarely detected in these creatures. Their actions and squeals seemed to be nearing a frenetic pitch! As Hero came upon the area, he felt himself being caught up in this excitement. He could feel the mutual pulsing of a single heart, he heard the thoughts of one united mind, and he could imagine the taste of blood of a victim as his agitation flourished into an insatiable feeding frenzy!

In the delirium that often accompanied this tumultuous feeling, Hero heard another sound that washed all of this aside.

He was not sure but it seemed to be the cry of the rats intended meal! But what was that sound? Hero listened more intently, his true instincts now steeled against those of his inherited ones as he focused in all sounds not in "rat." Was that the sound of a mobile unit? Those things, when you heard one that happened to be functioning, often made sounds indescribable to even the most intelligent of species. But this sound was one that Hero had heard before and it was not a mobile unit. Hero's pace quickened as he heard it again. Now racing at full speed, Hero knew what the sound was. As he sped towards the rats meeting place, he again heard the frightened cry of a very young Vertical.

The sound lead Hero into one of the partially demolished buildings that were so common on his planet since the last time the Verticals fought with each other. Into the bowels of it he ran as if their mythical great-evil were after him. Hero felt he had to help this small Vertical since they were the only type of its species that was uniformly kind to Hero and his own.

As the Verticals grew greater in their years most of them lost their compassion and innocence, the greatest of their qualities. It is true that some larger ones retained these feelings until the time of their death, but only in the young ones were they genuinely true.

Dodging in and out of great chunks of concrete that had fallen, Hero soon came to a room where part of the roof had caved in with the wall; a small shaft of sunlight shone through from the outside. In this musty light that pervaded the room Hero could see the figure of a small female Vertical. She was weeping almost imperceptibly. She seemed to be to the point of exhaustion. How long she had been in this place, Hero was unable to determine. She had apparently wandered in to this room, became ensnared in some debris, and did not have the intellect or physical attributes needed to free herself.

Hero surveyed her situation closer. He could see that a portion of the little Verticals outer garments had indeed become entangled with some particularly jagged portions of the fallen structure. The poor little things' hands had become cut and bloodied as she had attempted to free herself from her predicament. It was this smell of blood that had alerted the rats to her whereabouts and then to an understanding of her helplessness. The first animal had called for another then another then another, after a small pack of them had accumulated in the room they undoubtedly had enough collected intelligence to see that an easy meal was theirs for the taking. This blood lust multiplied with each rat within sensing distance and soon the pack had swelled in an obscene way. This mob behavior was one aspect of a rat's existence that raised Hero's ire.

Fortunately, in their frenzy, the gluttonous little beasts had not detected Hero. His borrowed instincts had also helped screen his presence as he crouched in a shadow trying to figure the best way to take on the enormous amount of rats that had now accumulated. He could see a few of them scurrying back and forth across the floor as the cowardly animals tested the area for safety, but Hero knew that the walls were teeming with them. Still they feared the little Vertical despite her situation.

But even as Hero watched, they became bolder. Soon more and more of them showed themselves through the holes in the wall where they hid. Hero knew he had to wait for just the right time. His element of surprise may be the only way either he or the little Vertical was going to survive this sure test of life and death.

Moments passed. One animal, which appeared to be the King Rat, kept emerging then retreating back into his hole. Each time he came out he came closer to his intended victim. Hero knew that it would soon be time to act and he also knew that the plan he had quickly devised must work! Again the leader emerged from his hollow, this time he came to an exposed part of the little Verticals flesh and sniffed it. As he turned to go back, his pace was less brisk, more self-assured. He stayed in his hole longer this time, no doubt making plans over how to divide the spoils with his hierarchy of henchmen. The next time he came out would be the time for Hero to strike.

Hero tensed his muscles. As he did he heard a few indistinct squeals from within the holes. Had the rats detected him? Would they now run in fear? No! They were now sharing a mob's bravado, the "safety in numbers" theory also held by so many Verticals. The brief panic that Hero had caused soon became swept under this tide of this collective boldness. In another moment, the lead rat emerged, his red eyes glowing in blood lust as he approached his helpless victim. Hero would guarantee that this would be the last thing this creature saw!

Just as the brute was about to draw the first droplet of the little Verticals vital fluid, Hero was upon him with a great piercing yowl that surely turned the other rat's bravery into so much false dreams. Hero sank his sharp teeth into the back of the King Rat's neck as he swung the creature about until he heard the snap of his neck. Releasing the King, he stood over the dead body in grim defiance.

This was an effective maneuver but Hero knew from inherited instincts that it would not be enough. He had to act fast. Once the King Rat was dead, Hero pounced on the little Verticals fallen form. His razor sharp teeth began to tear away at the outer garments that were entrapping her. These Verticals! Why did they need things such as these in the first place? But no time for philosophical meandering now! Hero knew that his time was short. Shock value could only last so long!

Hero managed to rip away the greatest portion of the garment that was holding the little Vertical with minimal effort. He then began to attack the second, and last, portion of the garment that was confining her, when he felt a pressure on his back. A rat was upon him and he had not noticed? No, it was only the hand of the little one. She was stroking him in the way that these creatures do. What a sweet dear thing this little one was. That she could show affection for a mangy old animal as himself in the face of such danger spoke well for the future of these Verticals. Hero purred.

But not for long. He heard a familiar shuffling from inside the wall as two of the more courageous rats emerged from their holes. They were undoubtedly courageous only because of their enormous size; put together they would almost be equal to Hero. Fortunately, they seemed to be imbeciles. It had to be a lack of intelligence that had kept them under the power of the now dead King Rat. They were most likely the next in the great one's chain of command. Giving a muscular idiot a high place of authority was the easiest way to ensure that he would not kill you since they felt that their position depended on your life. However, when that life ended, they were fearless in attaining a place in total power. In some ways, they were far more dangerous to Hero than the King, especially since Hero was no longer an unknown quantity!

Hero had to use his intelligence as an edge. He pounced on the first idiot, sinking his teeth deep into its muscular back. With some effort, Hero heaved the first rat into the face of the second idiot rat. The injuries to the first idiot and the surprise of the second idiot gave Hero the time he needed. He grabbed the second idiot and eliminated him is the same way he did the King rat. Before the damaged idiot could get away, Hero did the same to him. Again he yowled as his blood lust overtook him, challenging the entire pack in one suicidal gesture.

It took a few precious moments, but Hero gathered his wits and returned to the task at hand. A few more bites at some fabric then the little Vertical was free to leave.

But she did not! It may have been weariness or a lack of understanding of the danger that she was in that held in place. Instead of running, she now stroked old Hero while uttering soft phrases in a tone that he knew well. He did enjoy this. But there was no time now!

Since all their leaders and pseudo-leaders had fallen, anger began to swell amidst the rat's rank and file! The situation was beginning to look like all wars. No matter what started the altercation, it would be hate that perpetuated it and only death would end it.

Hero knew that he had to make the little Vertical move! So, for the sake of reason only, he scratched her. This made her bolt to a sitting position while screaming in pain and disbelief! Still she did not make a move to leave. Hero felt sorry for the little one, but he scratched her again. This time she made a move away from Hero, which was fine, except she was going towards the rats! With his strength ebbing, Hero vaulted to a place between her and the rat holes while hissing and yowling like an animal gone mad. It took every bit of his will, but Hero scratched little Vertical again. This time she ran in the direction of the opening in the wall where she had obviously entered.

Hero watched as the little Vertical retreated back out into a world where, though it was not much better, she had a greater chance of survival. Relief swept through Hero's old aching bones like a balm. He had not wanted to hurt the little Vertical but it had been mandatory that he expedite her departure from this rat-infested room. The rats!

As his thoughts returned to them, he felt a sharp pain between his shoulders. He swung around wildly until he was successful in bucking the little beast off him. When his eyes cleared of the pain, he stood motionless gazing into the army of red eyes that had emerged from the walls. Hero turned to run, but there was no where to go, he was surrounded by a sea of rats. Could he talk his way out of this scrape as he had done so often in the past? Doubtful. Could he fight his way out of this at his age? There was only one way to find out. Hissing and yowling he jumped into the fray.

As blood, flesh, and fur flew in every direction, Hero noticed that the little Vertical was now out of sight and completely safe. With this warm assurance in his mind and rats at every turn, he passed through The Portal.

*   *   *

Hero stood and stretched. He was not hungry. He was not cold. He was not unhappy. He was never any of these things in this new life-plane. He felt vibrant and young again! About the only time he had any problem was when he met up with any of the small animals that he had personally sent here before him. The little beggars were always thanking him for this service despite his assurances that this was just the natural order of things. Hero gazed around the beautiful golden land that was now his home. Despite missing the action of his last life-plane, Hero had no objections to this one. There was peacefulness here as he had never felt in any of his other existences. Hero wondered if this was the "last level" that so many animals speculated about?

There was only one way to find out, and that was to as he had always done, relax and see what Fate would deal him next. So, with nothing better to do, Hero lay back down and went to sleep.

THE END

JENNIFER RISING

The house was dark and quiet. Dad and mom snored softly in their room; Jeff rested peacefully in his bed just down the hall. All was serene, except for Jenny.

"Hurry, hurry! Get up, get up! Oh, get up will you? Get up. Why won't they get up? I wish they could understand me.", thought Jenny, her tail beating furiously.

"My boy, Jeff! He will understand. He is with me most of the time and he is big enough to help. I will go see him. He will understand, he will help."

"Mphshaw," Dad mumbled.

"Hmmphsee. What?", Mother asked, "What?".

"Nothing, nothing." Dad said, "It's just Jenny fussing. She probably wants to play."

"What time is it?"

"Too early to play." said dad, "Anyway, she ran into Jeff's room. He will see what she wants."

*   *   *

"Master, Master!! Get up, get up. Oh, the smell! It is so strong now! Get up, get up."

"Jenny!!", Jeff mumbled sleepily, "quit that barking and whining, it's too early to get up!"

"But you must get up, you must! Can't you smell it? I have been smelling it for a long time, now it smells dangerous. It is going to be bad for us all if we don't flee! Please get up! Please!!!!", she begged as she licked Jeff's face to arouse him.

"Oh, Jenny! Quit kissing me. I love you, but I want to sleep now."

"I love you too, Master, that is why you must get up. You must understand me. Oh, why do we have to be of different species? Why couldn't we have both been canines, then you would understand me when I talk to you?"

"I know I must be annoying you, but the danger is coming closer. I should have tried to tell you earlier, but I wanted you to get your rest, and I thought it might pass us by, but from the smell, it must be getting very close! You must get up."

"Look!! Look at the light outside!! Is it ever this light before dawn? I know the seasons are changing, but it is never like this at this time of the year."

"Jenny, get away from the window, girl."

"You must look!!"

"What is it Jenny, do you see, a jack rabbit or something?"

"No! It is not a leporidae! I would not be afraid of a leporidae. It is that thing that I am most afraid of. You know what it is, you have no fear of it, but I know how deadly it can be. I cannot frighten it away; it stalks us all without fear!! Come to the window, you must see, it approaches more quickly! Oh, why did I not wake you earlier?"

"Okay, Jenny what is it? Do you want me to look? Is that it girl, you want me to look?"

"He understands! He understands! Yes, come look, come look!"

"What is it girl? What is that light?"

"It is the fear that approaches!"

"Jenny! We have to go outside!"

"Yes. Go out, go out!"

*   *   *

The unusual calm of the morning told Jeff that all was not as it should be. He and Jenny had stood for many mornings on the porch of their house and listened to the forest awaken. Occasionally, Jenny would chase a bird or a rabbit for exercise. But today was different; there were no birds or rabbits, today only an eerie sound carried by the wind broke the stillness. Jeff scanned the horizon, now fully awake and alert. Jenny stood frozen, staring into the oncoming wind, ears up, nose sniffing frantically. For what Jeff did not know. Suddenly the unnatural light that he and Jenny had detected broke over a nearby hilltop showing Jeff the danger his family faced.

"Forest fire! There it is Jenny, coming over the ridge. Boy, the wind! I've never seen it blow like this, girl. It is so hot and fast, and it is bringing the fire right to our house. We have to wake mom and dad!"

*   *   *

"Get up, get up, get up!"

"Don't hit Jenny, dad. Get up! There is a fire headed our way. That is what she has been trying to tell us."

Dad sat bolt upright, he knew Jeff was not one to exaggerate. Quickly pulling on his robe, he looked outside, and then called a nearby Ranger station.

They confirmed that a fire had broken out, but the Ranger had not been aware that it was so close to any houses. He said he would send help immediately.

For what seemed like hours, but was not, the family stood on the porch and watched the flames. Jenny became more and more agitated as they approached.

"Listen dad! Sirens, planes! The fire fighters are on the way with an airborne unit; that must mean that the fire is out of control! My Scout leader told us that flying tankers were only brought in when men alone couldn't contain a fire."

Dad heard the sounds too. He heard the sirens and the drumming beat of a large plane's multiple prop engines. This could only mean Jeff was right; the situation must be very bad. It was time to act. He quickly told everyone gather what they could and load it into their truck. As they were doing so, a frantic pounding came to the door.

It was the Ranger dad had spoken to. He told them that the fire had broken out in a campground and confirmed that it was now out of control, being driven by hot Santa Ana winds. He ordered the family to evacuate immediately, but Dad refused. He said that he would stay and defend his home until the last second. Still, he wanted his wife and Jeff to go now before it was too late.

Mom then refused. No one had to ask Jeff and Jenny how they felt as they stood close together showing no signs of fear. The Ranger argued, but finally gave up seeing that he could not persuade the family to go. He left to warn others as the first contingent of fire fighters came to try and stop the relentless march of flame that threatened the family's home.

*   *   *

The rest of the morning was a blur. Jenny was everywhere, exhorting the actions of the fire fighters. When they fell back from the fight, exhausted and dehydrated, Jenny would lick their faces and nuzzle their hands as if she were thanking them for trying to save the house.

"Thank you, now go rest. You are tired. My master and his mother have cool water and hot brown liquid for you. They also have food. Go now, rest, and replenish your strength for the fear knows no weariness. It will not rest, but you must."

Despite Jenny's efforts, the fight seemed hopeless. One fire line would be dug and the fire would jump it. A new one was dug and the fire would jump it, too. The massive flying water tankers continued to dump water as fast as they could refill. Sometimes flying so low, that their rumblings shook the house.

So it went until midday. Dad was worn and haggard. The fire was now just 500 feet from the dream he had worked so hard to get for his family. It was only now then he conceded that all may soon be lost.

Jeff, as tired as his dad, had gone to his room with Jenny. He looked around at the possessions he had acquired in his short life and realized that they all might soon be gone, too. As he and Jenny curled up on the floor of his bedroom for what might be the last time, he appealed to nature to intervene and save them.

*   *   *

"The wind has turned!" a firefighter shouted.

Dad ran to see if this was true. It was! The men, revitalized by this reversal of events, fought the fire with new vigor. Three hours later, it was a quarter of a mile away from the house and looked like it would soon be controlled as it headed for a nearby stream.

When Dad heard the news, he ran and kissed Mom, then he went in search of his son. He found Jeff and Jenny cuddled under blanket on the floor of the bedroom fast asleep.

Dad smiled.

He was proud of his boy for not being afraid in the face of overwhelming danger and of course he was proud of Jenny who had awakened them to this peril.

She was the best friend his little family ever had.

THE END

ONE MINUTE HERO

"Why in hell bring one of those in here?" Sam thought. Up to this point, the droning of the school bus engine had made his thoughts listless. He was tired from running around with his young son, trying to get the days' chores completed before they caught the shuttle bus to the county fair.

More than likely he just imagined it. Besides, the man's coat only flashed open for a moment—still, it almost had to be one. Even though he had never handled one, these weapons they were quickly becoming the Derringers of the full automatic weapons field. Every time you saw accounts of a terrorist act on the network news, sure enough somebody would be holding a Uzi sub-machine gun. You could even go into toy stores and see great replicas of the damn things.

But why bring one here? This was bus taking people to the county fair. Could be the other man thought that this was a regular bus and he got aboard thinking that he could take it to a local gun shop. That must be it; he thinks that is a regular bus. But could that be possible? This was a small yellow school bus not a big RTD bus and it was picking people up in the middle of a mall parking lot, not at a regular bus stop. Mistaking this for anything other than what it was didn't seem likely. Anyway, if he was taking his gun to a shop, why would he hide it under his coat? Wouldn't he be carrying in a case or something? The only answer must be that he was hiding it for a reason.

Sam could feel the hair on the nape of his neck stand up as other thoughts came to him. Was there a gun show at this fair? No. They have held gun shows at the fairgrounds but not during the actual fair. Was it a toy gun? If that were so, then why would the man hide it beneath his coat? Was he afraid that the bus driver would think it was real and not let him on? If it were real would he care? Maybe he did not want the bus driver to see it just now. Maybe he wanted to show it to her when the bus was moving. Maybe he wanted to hijack the bus!

Talk about raging paranoia! Sam sighed. Too many nights spent in front of the television watching the news! Too many hours spent poring over the newspaper! If possible, too much imagination! He turned to take a look at the other man that he had so wrongly misjudged—and the paranoia gripped him again!

When their eyes met, Sam felt another chill go up his spine as he noted the vacant look in eyes of the other passenger. The man suddenly looked very familiar to him. His wild blonde hair, cropped short in military style, stood straight up. His smooth-skinned face was not only devoid of emotion it seemed incapable of showing any!

Sam had seen it all before. For five years before he was married, he had labored in the maximum security wing of a state mental hospital and that was where he had seen that man's face! Not this man's face in particular, but faces just like his were plastered on the bodies of institutionalized men with like minds! It was a face only the severest mental illness could create!

But now what should he do? Shout out his suspicions to everyone? No. That could start the other man off on a shooting spree; everyone on the bus could be killed including he and his son. That thought shook Sam. His son! He must save his son at all costs!

Sam turned back to look at his boy who was oblivious to all terror including that which may have just boarded the bus. James sat squirming impatiently wanting the bus to start moving so he could go to the fair and pet the baby goats, but letting the bus start moving was something that Sam could not allow no matter what since that could be just what the other man wants. Once in motion he could command a detour to hell if he cared to. Sam could not allow that, he had to do something. He had to take a chance!

Picking up his son, he started out of the bus. Half way down the aisle, the boy started to protest loudly. Sam could feel the eyes of the other man on the his back. Was he reaching for the Uzi? Should Sam turn to look? What does he do in any case? Best to just freeze it out! A hand over the boy's mouth, reassuring words in his ears, promises of sweet things once outside of the danger zone; anything so as not to light the fuse of the other man! Now they were at the steps. He mumbled excuse to the bus driver, stepped out the door, and scuttled around the other side of the small postal service kiosk that was serving as a passenger pick up spot. A wave of relief engulfed Sam as he collapsed, shaking and holding his son close to him.

James began to squirm in his arms. He wanted to get back on the bus and go to the fair to see the baby goats and baby pigs. He wanted to know why they got off. The he began to cry thinking he did something wrong. Sam's thoughts were racing now! How do you keep a four year old occupied while you risk your life to save the rest of the people on the bus? Risk his life?

Yes, there was no question on that matter. To let the bus go with a possible mad man on board carrying an Uzi and the rest of the passengers facing death was something Sam could never live with. It would be far better to be wrong and look like a fool then to do nothing and face the guilt for the rest of his life. But what can an unarmed do in the face of such a threat?

First, he had to settle down his boy. Fishing in the pockets of his coat, Sam brought out a package of mini-doughnuts that he had been saving as a surprise. The sight of them and a few calming words caused James cries to subside. He told his son to eat all that he liked, until he got back. Daddy had to go talk to the bus driver for a few minutes. Will the boy be good? Childish promises did little to assure Sam. Still, at the moment, it would have to do.

Sam stood on shaky legs and reached into his left hand pants pocket. Yes! It was there! He wasn't sure he had brought the large box cutting knife that he used in his work, but luckily, even on his day off, he had absent-mindedly put it where it usually was five days a week.

Why? Did something tell him there would be a life and death need for it today?

No time for metaphysical meandering now! Sam had a job to do. With his son starting on the second of six doughnuts, he headed back to the bus, the knife now open and tucked into his inside coat pocket.

Time to fake it! He stumbled back on board calling for his son. Asking the bus driver if she had seen him, the driver looked puzzled. But there was no time to explain. Sam has to improvise as best he could! He had to keep calling for his son! He must pretend that the boy wandered away from him. That's it! Look in all the seats, calling, calling. Damn! If only he could act better! Was he being convincing enough? So far, as Sam approached his quarry, no sign had come to the man's face to show that he was suspicious. But this was a man who was possibly quite disturbed. Would he show any emotions at all or would he just open fire? No time to guess now. Sam had to keep up the act, slowly approaching his intended victim. Now, one more step, and he was past him. Still acting as the other man's eyes followed him. Is he convinced? Does he care? No time to determine this. He had to get on with it!

As his right hand slipped the knife out of his coat, his left fell over the other man's eyes holding them shut. Now the knife was at the man's throat, the tip pressing hard into the pit between the two jugulars. The suspect started to reach into his coat, but Sam shouted a warning of death and pulled back hard against the his neck, freezing his captives' hands in midair. Screams are rampant; pandemonium threatened to break loose. Now Sam shouted at the others as well. They must sit down! They must sit down and be quiet! Now! He must have time to think!

In a minute, maybe more, all is quiet except the sobs of those unaware of the real terror. Sam's mind is a cobweb of fear and confusion. Now what? What would a policeman do? How should a possibly misguided furniture salesman act in accordance? Nothing to do now except to calm down and clear his mind. His captive's hands still hung frozen in the air like a marionette that had lost its strings. An answer came to Sam in a crackle of static. Of course! The bus has a two-way radio on board!

First, clear the bus. Sam shouted the order but no one moved, he knew they were terrified, so he shouts the order again. Still no movement. The fools. Don't they realize he only wants to save them? The other man's hands begin to shake at this order so Sam commanded him to place them on the top of the seat in front of him. A little more pressure on the knife blade made the man reluctantly comply.

So, no one will leave. Now what? He calls to the bus driver and orders her to summon help. Have another driver call the police. This command seems to calm the rest of the people on the bus. Maybe now they will get off the bus. Sam tells them to do so once again and this time a few people in front start to do as they were told. He hears the driver also comply with his orders; soon the police would be on their way.

The trickle of people soon turns into a flood then a stampede as they each try to beat the other one off the bus. While still holding his captive in his grip, Sam feels for them. He too would like to runoff the bus. As the last person leaves he hears his son's voice outside. He is calling for his daddy, he is crying. Sam shouts to the bus driver to get his son and not let him get back on the bus, under no circumstances let him back on the bus!

Now the all the seats are empty save for the ones occupied by Sam and his prisoner. The sound of his son's crying voice intermingles with that of the other sobbing children. So far, Sam's captive has said nothing. Despite the other man's position, Sam could not detect any sign of fear from him. He did not tremble, he did not cry out, he was stone. Cold and hard. Sam knew the type, he had seen them before in the mental hospital. They would kill you just as soon look at you. They had no fear. They had no emotions of any kind. Sometimes these men were caught, convicted, and rightfully put to death. But increasingly they were let off because of their mental incapacity. They were condemned to life in a hospital to be cared for like prize animals while psychiatrists studied them. The sicker the deed, the more they were made into "celebrities" in the psychiatric world. Their victims should have it so good!

Sam did not want this one to get away. One inch up and one inch over would make the knife blade do its work and justice would be done. But what kind of justice is that? Who was this man that he was holding anyway? A terrorist? A psychopath? A completely innocent person? Sam's mind was feverish as sirens shattered his thoughts.

He soon could hear policemen herding the passengers away for the bus. His son was going with them. The people were telling the police the details of past few minutes. Presently there was silence.

Sam heard one of the police officers board the bus, crouching behind the barrier in front of the first seats. She demanded that Sam throw down his weapon and surrender!

She thought that he was the hijacker! He had to show her that she was wrong without letting the other man get to his gun—if he indeed did have one. If he let that happen, many people could still die. There was only one thing to do.

Sam ordered his prisoner to stand up with his hands in the air. A little more pressure on the knife blade showed him that he had better do as told. With both men now standing Sam pushed the assumed terrorist down the aisle towards the voice from that still hid behind the cover. Possibly thinking that she was going to be attacked, the officer ordered him to halt.

Sam did not comply. Instead he started to tell her what was really going on, that he was not a terrorist, that he was stopping a terrorist, or at least he thought he was. Sam had to be given time to explain all this after the got off the bus. But the officer did not want this to happen. Suddenly she emerged from behind the partition with gun drawn she repeated her demand. This stopped Sam from advancing, but he did not drop his weapon. He tried to tell the officer, now that they were face to face the real story. By cocking her gun, the officer showed that she did not know what to believe.

Now Sam had to do as told. If he resisted and the officer shot the other man, the bullet would surely pass through him and kill them both. Besides, the officer had them both covered at a short range, the other man would not dare to try anything.

He tossed his knife aside.

As the blade cleared the man's throat, his hands dropped to his coat. Sam dove behind a seat. A shot and the short, erratic burst of an automatic weapon followed. A heavy object fell across Sam legs, and all was quiet once more save the renewed sobs of the children outside the bus. Somewhere in a haze of his over heated mind Sam could hear his son crying.

Heavy hands gathered Sam up as handcuffs were put roughly on his wrists. He was shoved down the aisle and off the bus. On the way he looked back and saw the dead body of the other man. In his grip was an Uzi. The scene reminded Sam of that often quoted line, " . . . from my cold dead hands . . ."

The bright sunlight blinded Sam. When the ordeal had started, it had been foggy and gray, but now that overcast had burnt off and Sam realized that it was still early morning, less than fifteen minutes had passed since his ordeal began. It seemed more like an eternity.

From out of the nearby crowd, his son came running. He was crying as he clutched Sam's leg. Mercifully, the boy was allowed in the back of the waiting patrol car with him. There Sam assured his son that everything was fine. Daddy was unhurt and the bad man had gone away. As he spoke Sam hoped that he was telling the truth, for as of yet, the police had few words for him.

They sat in the back of the car for at least an hour as uniformed officers, detectives, and the coroner looked over the shooting scene. Many hushed words were spoken between these men and to others on police radios. Sam could see the passengers from the bus being interviewed, then released. But none of them were leaving. Sam figured it was just the morbid curiosity that abounds in most men. There was a body to see, so stay around and see it. To his surprise the body was removed yet they still stayed on.

By now his son was sleeping, the boy's head was cradled on Sam's lap. He wanted to hug his son so bad he could feel the boy in his arms, but his steel manacles prevented him for doing so. Sam was starting to get a little scared. What if the police decide to arrest him on some charge? Would he ever see his boy again? What could they charge him with anyway? He had not done anything wrong. He was about to pound on the glass of the window and demand some answers, when the door suddenly opened!

His son was awakened and, for a moment, Sam thought that his fears were turning to reality, but the officer's hands that had previously been so rough were now gentle as they helped Sam out of the patrol car. Then the crowd, which had swelled, to much more than just the bus riders, did something very odd indeed. They cheered.

They cheered even louder as the police removed the hand cuffs from Sam.

In the rush of people that gathered around, the crowd's behavior became understandable. A police detective explained to Sam that the other man on the bus was an escaped convict who had been serving time for numerous counts of assault, and, much to Sam's personal satisfaction, the detective told him that the other man had also spent a few years in the state hospital due to uncontrollable periods of paranoia. Why he had boarded the bus and where he got the Uzi may never be known, but it was felt, by the authorities, that the man was on the verge of doing something tragic. That made Sam a hero.

"Okay", thought Sam as he was thanked and congratulated from all sides, "this is all real fine. But I guess now I will have to wait until tomorrow to go to the fair."

THE END

SUPER HERO

I just wish that someone could tell me why stuff like this has to happen to me? While they're at it, they can tell me why it always has to happen in front of witnesses? Yes, I'm whining, but I mean, if it weren't for all those meddling people, I would have been able to pass the incident off as an overactive hangover, but no, they had to say they saw something fantastic happen and gum up the works. It was just fortunate for me that they changed their stories before the cops showed up.

It would've been real bad for me if everyone admitted that they knew what happened out there today since, in my profession, you can't draw too much attention to yourself. Getting your face plastered all over the newspapers and TV is the last thing that I need. Someone might see my face and think that I sure look like that phony Bank Examiner who came to see them last week, or that I sure looked like their old Aunt Tillie's last boy friend; the one that absconded with half of her worldly possessions.

Besides, if people knew what really happened, I might have to start acting differently. I wouldn't be able to just lay around all day figuring out ways to cheat good, honest, hard working, people out their money—an enterprise that I have been pursuing for most of my 43 years. I'm good at it, too. I am so good that I've never thought about doing anything else. The cops haven't been able to nail me on anything, and the people I take the money from usually can afford to lose it—which is why they lose it—so they don't complain too much. I consider myself to be an "honest" thief. I never steal from people who really need their money.

Today's madness started and ended so soon that even now I have a hard time believing that anything happened at all. When I recall the incident, it is as if I was seeing it in a dream, one of those dreams that are so substantive that you have a hard time figuring out what was real and what was the dream. Sitting here in my one-room apartment holding the police report, I can't deny the reality it represents, no matter how much I want to.

For now I've got to sit back and go over everything, I need to examine it from start to finish, that is the only way that I will ever be able to comprehend what actually happened.

The day started innocently enough as I was on my way to Mrs. Mallardo's house; she being a well-off, recently widowed lady of 87 years. She had just taken the bait on the tired but sure-fire bank examiner scam and I was nervous, as usual, about the operation. This was good because when I am nervous, I stay on my toes, just in case I have to make a quick exit. It may have been that I became overly absorbed by the day's operation. I may have been concentrating on it so much that I was not paying as much attention to my driving as I should have been. For whatever reason, I did not see the kid race in front of my car until what I thought was going to be too late.

Mrs. Mallardo's house was in a part of town that I wasn't too familiar with. She lived in a nice middle-class area with median priced homes that weren't anything like the lower income housing I had become accustomed to when I was growing up. It is a very pleasant neighborhood. Children were playing in yards; retirees were out planting roses or cutting the grass. Animals roamed, leash less, each knowing which home was their own.

I was taking all this in while looking for Mrs. Mallardo's house number when everything happened. Evidently a ball that this kid was playing with escaped his grasp and rolled into the street. It was only because I saw the top of his head over the hood of my car that I was able to react at all.

In my mind now, the play of events is like those slow-motion dream sequences that you see so often in the movies. I saw his head and I hit the brakes hard. This could not have taken more than a second, yet in my memory, it seemed like it took two minutes. I thought the kid was dead. Then it happened.

In my panic I pulled back on the steering wheel of my car as if it were an airplane that I was trying to take to a greater altitude. In that second, I wished that I could raise the car up and over the kid—and that is exactly what happened; or so all of us at the scene first thought.

The front end of my car reared up and wheeled to the left as if I was riding a horse and had to pull up short at a barrier. Miraculously, my car came down free and clear of the kid.

I lay with my head on the steering wheel, thinking about the bloody scene that had to be outside of my car as people came running into the street. Amazingly, the kid's mother had picked him up and was hugging him. She was crying in a state of anguish and relief, not sure weather she should laugh or cry, only happy that her kid was still alive!

I was ecstatic, but I also wanted to leave. I realized that I needed to drive on. Get away from there as quickly as I could. I surely didn't need this type of distraction. However, the others who came running to the scene prevented my exit. One older gentleman was knocking on the window of my car, clearly wishing to check me for injuries since I had again put my head on the steering wheel. Someone else shouted that they had called for the police and an ambulance, unaware that no one was hurt. If I had driven off at that point, someone would surely have reported my license number to officers arriving on the scene and they would have issued a warrant with my name on it for leaving the scene of an accident—although no accident actually occurred. I couldn't afford this kind of inquiry. So, I had no choice but to get out of the car.

When I did I was surrounded by several people who had witnessed the event. They marveled at my driving skills; amazed that I was able to avoid the kid. They began to inquire about how I managed to raise the front end of my car up, as I had evidently done. One man swore that the car had risen at least five feet in the air. This talk went on for a few more minutes before the reality of what these speculations truly meant. As the weight of their words circulated among them, an uneasy quiet began to spread through the group. All at once, I was no longer a hero in their eyes; to the contrary, I was someone they needed to fear and puzzle over. It was an awkward moment that lasted no longer than that, a moment, but like all the other events of the day, it seemed like an eternity.

I remember being able to look into each person's eyes; I could read their thoughts. An older lady who stood mumbling quietly to herself obviously thought I must be an angel for only the heavenly sent could do what I did. A teen-age boy, eyes bright with hope and curiosity, saw me as a superman, the one who would save the world for his generation. A man, who looked close to my age, was giving the events a more analytical view. His eye's first examined the front end of my vehicle, then the street section that we were standing on, and finally they turned to me as if he were gauging the amount of strength I possessed. What conclusions he drew, he kept to himself.

No one spoke as each person stood alone in their thoughts. We might have stood there for all eternity had not the sound of approaching sirens broken the silence. The young mother was the first to move as she came forward to hug me, be I devil or angel; she felt that it was my actions that saved her child. I could tell that the others, though amiable, still held forward doubt. All through the process of making the police report and assuring the ambulance drivers that no injuries had been incurred, I felt as if I they avoided me. All of the witnesses appeared to wish that I would just leave their neighborhood as quickly as possible so they could go back to their normal lives that were free from miracles and the like.

The final report said this: I had been able to avoid hitting the kid by quickly stepping on my brakes and swerving to the left. The police, and now the witnesses who kept what they really saw to themselves, gradually left while considering me a hero of some sort. What they left me with was the mystery I am now trying to work through.

For the past few hours I have been trying to understand all of this, because even with my sanity's urgent need to follow my doubts, I have to face the fact that I know what really happened: I somehow raised the front end of my car solely by the force of my mind. As I realized this, I also realized that this was not an accident. I have the power to do this.

Just a moment ago, I raised my dining table, then my bed, my television, and then all three of them at once. I have full confidence that I could raise my apartment building from its roots if I wished. There seems to be no limit to my newfound power.

So what does this make me? Am I to follow the belief of the old woman who thinks I am an angel, or am I as the teen seemed to have thought—a super hero? Perhaps I should view myself in the analytical way as the man my age did. Maybe I am just a person who possesses newly found advanced telekinetic powers that were triggered by the events of the day; someone for the scientific world to examine and dismiss.

I've never been one given to religious feelings. If there is a God out there, He knows this. So why he would endow me with any special gifts at this late date would be something theologians could debate for time eternal. No, I am an unlikely angel.

A superman I am sure that I am not. For one thing, my physique does not allow me to wear anything more close fitting than a sweat-shirt. If I went out in tights, I know that I would be arrested no matter how good my intentions are. Besides, too much do-gooding would make me gag.

The thought of scientists probing me was extremely repugnant. I've never having been one given to academics, yet I have managed to become a clear thinking, fairly well spoken man, despite having been asked to leave the premises of several halls of academia. No, I couldn't allow myself to become a lab rat for any pseudo-intellectual pencil pushers. They would never be able measure my powers in terms they could explain anyway, so they would point out my chosen profession while saying I was just trying to pull of another fraud.

So now what? None of the options open to me sound pleasing, but my eliminating them leaves few other choices about what I can do if I am to keep my sanity. Since no one will admit to what they saw, especially me, I suppose I'm just going to have to do what I have to do and that is to forget the whole thing and get back to work.

Now, where the hell did I put Mrs. Mallardo's phone number? There it is. Hmmm . . . . now how should I explain my delay in arrival? Perhaps a bank robbery? Yeah, that's it! I will tell that I had to stop a bank robbery. I will tell her that a man came in the bank wearing a ski-mask, carrying a big gun, and began demanding money. I came up on him from behind and managed to disarm him using my advanced karate training. Yes, that's it. She would think of me as hero and trust me even more. Now where is that address?

THE END

ADVENTURE

THE TREASURE OF ARROYO SECO

Jackson spit the accumulated trail dirt in his mouth on to the trail dirt beneath his feet. There was little difference in the color. He needed water, and he needed it badly.

Now he was almost sorry he tried to help that old hombre he came across on road a few miles back.

He was pretty much dead from dehydration when Jackson found him anyway, but his mama always taught him to help those less fortunate than himself, so he shared his sorry little supply of water with the old hombre after he had drug him into the shade of a rocky outcropping. He had died clutching Jackson's shirt while apparently thanking him for his kindness.

His final action, before he passed on, still had Jackson puzzling. With his last bit of strength he managed to dig a scrap of paper out from under his faded brown serape and press it into Jackson's hand. He kept trying to tell Jackson about the paper. He acted as if it were something real special. The word he kept using over and over again was one that Jackson knew despite his limited knowledge of the Spanish language.

"Tesoro, mi amigo", he had rasped as he died. "Tesoro . . . encuentralo." His eyes implored Jackson to take the paper. As he did so, the old hombre died.

Jackson had buried him where he lay, in the shade of the rock. He had used his knife to etch a makeshift headstone for the old man into the side of the hill. He wrote a one word in tribute to the man's courage; it was the one word the old hombre spoke that he knew the meaning of: Treasure. Now it looked as if it were Jackson's burden to finish the hunt that the old man had started, because what the old hombre had given him was clearly a map of some kind.

Though he didn't understand the words written on it, from the symbols, Jackson figured there was a town not too far up ahead, but whether he and his horse could make it, he didn't know. They plodded on under the merciless desert sun.

The heat rose up from the desert floor in waves reaching for the sky. At times he felt as if they were going to lift him up with them, and at times, he was ready to let go and just drift away on them.

Jackson laid his head on the soaking mane of Stella, his mare. She was a beauty and she was his best friend. He was angry at himself for bringing her with him. He could have sold her and let her live out a peaceful life on any of the ranches he passed as he fled south to the border of Mexico. He could have picked up another horse, one that would have done the job, yet not one who would be a friend like Stella. But in his fear, he did not want to be alone. Bringing her into this hell hole was a purely selfless act.

He had fled in a panic, ashamed at the thing he'd done and afraid of the retribution that he felt would surely face if caught.

In starving desperation, he had robbed a drifter of some food and a little money with his empty gun. Now he just knew that the law was after him. He imagined a huge posse of men, toting six guns and Winchesters fully loaded, sitting astride massive steeds, with hoofs thundering beneath them in pursuit of his skinny carcass. All were ready to lynch him the minute they caught him. Being a first time thief, he didn't realize that this sort of thing rarely happened unless you were a murderer and then only if you killed someone that somebody cared about. In reality, no one was looking for Jackson. The drifter never reported the robbery since he was wanted for crimes much worse than the one Jackson had pulled off.

The trail seemed to go on forever. Stella never strayed, but her breathing was heavy and foam was beginning to form around her nostrils. Jackson finally dismounted and led his poor loyal beast.

Soon his head began to spin, his vision blurred yet he hung on to consciousness. He thought could see buildings not too far off, but were they real or were they mirages caused by an overheated mind? No matter, he had to press on towards them. One foot followed the other, mindless in their actions.

He came to a door, reached for it and pitched forward, face down in the dirt. He could go on no more. He closed his eyes and waited for death to take him away while hoping that Stella would find water and survive his foolishness.

*   *   *

It was cool in this place. Wetness hooded his face. He was submerged in a watering hole, swimming upwards towards the light. He opened his aching, sun burnt eyes to see only clouds. Was he dead? His hands went to his eyes and pulled the damp white cloth off his face only to find that he was staring into the face of an angel. So this was Heaven?

"Madre, ven a ver. Ha despertado", the angel called out.

A stout woman with tightly wound gray hair entered the room at the beckoning.

"Si, Dio lo ha salvado", the woman replied as she stooped over to examine Jackson's face. When she began to poke and prod him, Jackson came to the realization that he was still alive and that the angel and the older lady must have been the reason why.

"I don't understand your lingo, ma'am, but I sure thank you for helping me out."

The angel and the old lady looked at each other for a moment. Finally the angel gave this terse assessment: "Gringo".

"Yes ma'am. I am a gringo. I come down from the Arizona territory, looking for work." he lied half-heartedly.

Again, the angel looked at the old lady. Again she gave her terse assessment: "Bandito".

Jackson was taken back by this word—another one of the few Spanish words he knew. The look on his face must have said something to the old lady, who turned to the angel and corrected her: "Bandito pequeño".

Whatever that meant, the two women burst out laughing.

He laughed with them and felt more human than he had in a long time. He liked his saviors.

The angel held out her hand. "My name is Raquel Deseo. This is my mama, Julia. We are happy to see you are alive, 'bandito pequeño' or not."

"Well I'd be lying if I didn't say I was more than glad to be here, but tell me where is 'here'. Where am I?"

Raquel turned and translated his question to her mama. Mama shook her head and clucked some words he did not understand.

"You are in Arroyo Seco, strange one. You came here not knowing where you were going? Maybe you are a bandito grande after all?"

"No ma'am, if I understand you, I am not a big crook. I am a small, foolish one at best. I was hungry and lost in the outback of Arizona; I didn't even have bullets left to shoot some food. So I robbed another trail bum with my empty gun. Then I headed south. I figured the law, if there were any to be found, would be after me for sure."

Raquel looked into his still hazy eyes as if trying to ascertain if there was any truth in his words. Apparently satisfied, she smiled again.

"I understand you fleeing blindly into a foreign land and getting lost, but what lead you here."

"Just chance, ma—"

"Please call me Raquel."

"Uh, just chance, Raquel. I really didn't know where I was going. I got on this long trail thinking there had to be water somewhere on it but I was wrong. I went on for miles and miles, nursing my canteen until it was almost dry. My poor horse—Stella! Did you find a horse? She is my horse Stella. I hoped she got found even as I though I was dying. Did you find her?"

"Calm down senor gringo. We found a horse standing over you. We reasoned she was yours. She is outside with water and some hay to eat. She is fine. Horses are stronger, and often smarter, than their owners. You are lucky to have such a loyal animal. If mama and I had not seen her standing still in the distance, we might not have gone to see why she was doing this. We would never have found you in time."

"Jackson. My name is Jackson."

"Well Mr. Jackson, tell us the rest of the story that brought you to our dusty little villa."

"Beg pardon Raquel, Jackson's my first name. Like I was saying, I was almost out of water, when I came across an old hombre lying across his dead horse. He was darn near dead himself, but I put him under some shade and gave him the last few drops I had. He died anyway, but not before he gave me this".

Jackson fished the tattered map he had been given out of his hip pocket. "Don't know why, but the old hombre seemed to think it was worth something. He said some words I didn't understand, but it seemed like he wanted me to follow the map, like it would lead me to something. He kept saying the word 'tesoro'."

Raquel took the paper from Jackson's hand. As she studied it, she muttered some of the words on the paper. Louder, she muttered, "El tonto! El viejo tonto!"

Then she burst into tears, so violent that Jackson wanted to sit up and hold her close to him. But he could not summon the strength. He had never seen an angel cry before and the sight of it disturbed him to no end.

Her mama came running at the sound of her sobs. She held her close and asked her, repeatedly, a question in Spanish. Finally the beautiful angel was able to quell her weeping long enough to say a few words while holding out the map.

Now it was mama's turn to wail—if possible—louder than Raquel had wailed. Jackson could stand no more of this. What grief had he brought on to these two kindly women? He wanted to flee and leave them to their quiet life.

Unsteadily, he pulled himself up in bed. The women, in their sorrow, took no notice of him. He stood, took two steps towards the door, and crashed down to the floor in a wave of blackness.

*   *   *

The next time he awoke, the blackness did not fade away. It was night time and much cooler. He found that sitting up was easier, so he tried standing. Still shaky, but able to take a pace or two, Jackson decided to sneak out in the middle of the night. He could not face his saviors again—the memory of the pain he caused them was going to live with him for a long time.

His boots and shirt had been taken off of him. The thought of this caused him mild embarrassment at the chance the beautiful Raquel had disrobed him so. Shuffling around in the dim moonlight that filtered in through a nearby window, he found his boots under the bed and his shirt airing over the back of a chair. As quietly as possible, he made ready to go.

Stepping lightly, he found the front door. It creaked noisily has he opened it. Stopping, he listened for sounds of the angel and her mama. Nothing stirred, so he gave the door one swift shove causing a loud, but brief, report. He stepped swiftly through it only to find Raquel sitting on the porch.

She sat on a rickety looking chair, not seeming to notice him. He stepped quietly, he thought, not sure what to do next, when Raquel spoke, "So, you will leave us? In the middle of the night like a bandito on the run?"

"No Raquel", Jackson responded, slightly offended. "I will leave before I bring you and your wonderful mother more grief. I could not stand to see the two of you crying anymore. I should not have come here."

Raquel stood and approached him.

"I believe you, Jackson. You are no criminal. No criminal could make such a statement." She put her hand to his cheek and it felt as if a feather had touched him. Angel wings? Her skin was so soft and smelled so fresh. He put his hand up and held hers against his face. He turned and kissed it lightly. She let it linger a moment longer, looking deeply into his eyes. They must have reflected the mixture of pain and pleasure that he was now feeling.

Removing her had, she said, "It was not you who caused the pain, Jackson. It was that old fool that you acted so kindly towards. He was my father."

Jackson could not speak. He stepped back, stumbling off the edge of the porch, and looked up at the stars so bright in the desert sky. His mama had believed in one religion or the other, but he had never been convinced by any of them. Still, now as he gazed at the heavens, he had to wonder what kind of force, if any, was at play. How had he made his way on to this trail, found that old hombre, and then, in desperation, why had he followed the map that eventually lead him to this house and this beautiful woman. It was if he were being guided along each step of the way. What could happen next?

"You look at the sky, Jackson? Do you question God on some matter?"

"Not necessarily question, Raquel. Just wonder . . ."

"How it is you came to this place at this time?"

Jackson was startled at her ability to read his thoughts.

"Don't be shocked Jackson. I often ask the same question. I would like to leave the dusty hole of Arroyo Seco and see the rest of the world. But I stay for reasons I do not yet know."

"It is so beautiful tonight, Raquel. So cool and clear. Maybe you stay through the hell of the days to visit the heaven of the nights?"

"So poetic, Jackson. I would think you could do better than rob men for a living."

At that Jackson spun on his heel, determined to leave, to be on his way, but Raquel immediately knew she had spoken wrongly. She reached out and touched his shoulder.

"Forgive me, please! I know you are not a bandito. You are too kind and too well spoken. Sometimes men have to do what they think is right, even if it seems wrong to all others. My father was just such a man."

"Tell me about him", Jackson said as he turned back to the beautiful angel.

"Come sit. I cannot stand and speak of his folly. It is too painful."

Jackson held her hand as they took a seat on the large bench that took up most of the small porch. If she noticed at all, she did not seem to mind.

"At one time our villa flourished. Our small stream ran blue with water. We were known as Aqua Dulce then. Men worked the fields while women and children worked at processing what they grew. I remember doing this when I was a child. Then, slowly, the flow of the river began to lessen. Men blamed the relentless heat, but we knew it was not the heat. The heat had been here since before men came to know this land. No one knew what was killing the river and our village.

Men fought with each other for rights to the water. Some were killed. More moved away, abandoning the homes they had known since childhood. Too soon the water stopped completely. My father, and few others, dug in the dirt looking for wells. We were fortunate to have found one on our land. The output is not much, but we can grow a little food, raise some chickens, and see to our basic needs. But the pitiful little well is also starting to show signs of drying up. Some days there is no water at all. This disturbed my father. He did not want to leave his home. He wanted his grandchildren to grow up where he did."

With that said, Raquel began to tear up. The wetness, so precious in her little village, made her beautiful brown eyes glisten. They were never lovelier.

Jackson wiped away a tear that ran down her cheek and pulled her head onto his shoulder. Her dark hair smelled sweet to him. He had not held that many women in this manner. She stayed there for a moment, composing herself. Then she pulled back.

"So he left. He said the federale's should know about this tragedy. They should know that a town is dying and they should come and help in some way. So he left to find these mysterious men-who-know-all, not knowing where he was going or who he was seeking.

Mama begged him not to leave, but he would not listen. He was going to find help if it killed him—which it did. He was fool and mama knew that when he left he would never return."

Jackson had been listening to the sad tale, not sure how to respond, not having the words to reply. But the last thing Raquel said interested him.

Desperate to make her feel better, he said, "Raquel, you're right, he did not make it back to the village. But he *was* coming home, or so it seemed. Why else would he be on the same trail that lead me to your town?"

Raquel sat up straight. Jackson could tell that she was poring over this possibility.

He went on, "Your father does not sound like the kind of man who would come back in defeat. Maybe he found help after all!"

Hope glimmered, and then faded in Raquel's eyes.

"But he died. We will never know." She began to cry again.

"Wait Raquel," Jackson said, as he lifted her head so he could look into her eyes, "That map that he gave me. He seemed to think it was very valuable. He kept saying something about treasure. What was on it?"

"I did not look at it closely. It looked liked an official document of some kind. Mama and I recognized his handwriting on it. That is how we knew it was he who you found in the desert." Her hand gave Jackson's face a light, almost loving, caress as she said this.

"I was going to leave tonight, Raquel. I couldn't bear to be in the same house with you and your mama after delivering so much grief to it, but now I will stay the night if you still will let me."

"Of course, Jackson, we did not want you to leave. You brought no misery here. You only passed on, innocently, the message that caused our anguish."

He hugged Raquel close to him, briefly.

"Okay then, in the morning, I want to look at that map a little closer."

*   *   *

Dawn broke over the desert floor, lighting up the dew drops on the barrel cactus as if they were jewels adorning the heads of the kings and queens of the desert. Mighty Saguaros towered in hushed sentinel before the diminutive royalty.

Jackson stood and stretched enjoying the coolness that had only a trace of the heat the day would bring. He smelled food cooking in the next room and realized that he was famished. The last time he had eaten had been—when? He wasn't sure, but he new he had to eat soon or die of starvation.

As he dressed he fingered his holster with the empty pistol in it, and then thought better of wearing it to the table. He turned and followed the aroma.

Mama looked up from her stove and smiled. She waved him to a place at the table where he found coffee, bread, and honey. Forgetting his manners, he dove into the offerings like the starving man he was. After his third slice of bread, he heard sweet laughter behind him. It was Raquel.

Looking lovelier than ever, she admonished him, "Slow down senor gringo Jackson. You will not have room for mama's eggs. That is a meal many men would die to have."

"Don't you worry about that, Raquel. I will not only eat the eggs, I will eat the whole chicken coop if you let me at it."

Raquel translated this for her mama. This brought out a burst of laughter then a torrent of words he did not understand, but seemed to indicate that she would beat him silly if he so much as looked at a chicken.

He stood and bowed, "Tell mama that I would never touch a feather on any of her prized egg layers and that I would knock any man on the head who tried to do so."

Raquel did as he asked. Mama brought over a plate of eggs to him and set it on the table as if in triumph. Then she smiled and gave him a quick hug while looking at Raquel before she turned back to her cooking.

Raquel joined him at the table, bringing the map with her.

She looked over it purposely now, as if she really were in search of treasure. Finishing his delicious eggs that were scrambled with a mixture of flavored meat in them, Jackson was curious as hell about what she was discovering in the words written on it.

"What does it say, Raquel?"

"I do not understand all of the words, but this is not 'tesoro' as my father wrote here. This is just some kind of federale document. He must have obtained it from a government source somewhere that he traveled. The place of origin is not stated on the map—and yes it is truly a map of some kind. But what kind, I do not know. It looks a little like a diagram of the area around our village, but this name is not one that that is known to me. It says 'Tierra de Esperanza'— the land of hope."

Jackson followed the trail etched on the map, in his blurry memory of the day before, he vaguely remembered the road twisting this way and that, almost exactly as it was drawn out. Could the town have had another name?

"I'm not too smart, Raquel, but I might know what some of the words mean. My mama always made me read everything and anything she could get a hold of."

Raquel looked doubtful, but went on, "This word is in here a lot, see along the edges, it says something like 'meridian'. I think it refers to these lines on the page. But I cannot tell. All the lines do not go from one side to the other.

The word 'water' is here, here, here, here, and here. Five spots." She said, pointing at each location on the map.

"That means there is water in those places, Raquel?"

"At one time, perhaps, but as far as I can tell, the spots are in the middle of the arroyo, the now dry arroyo where the river once ran. As it dried up, the men changed the name of our town to what it is now. They were bitter over the path that fate had taken them."

"What other words are there, Raquel?"

"Nothing unusual. Just words, but one is like it does not belong here, so odd it seems."

"What is it?"

"Do not laugh, Mr. Gringo Jackson," she said as she flashed her dazzling smile, "I am not sure of the translation, but it says 'arm' and I think 'upper', but I am not sure."

Jackson grinned widely. His face lit up in such a way that Raquel thought he was going to stand up and shout in joy.

"Could it say 'forearm', my little angel?"

She gave him a troubled stare. Then looked at the map again. In a moment she spoke, "Yes, that could be the word."

"Then do not look unhappy, Raquel. This could be more 'tesoro' than you think. I believe I know what this is."

Still she looked troubled.

"Why do you look so?" Jackson finally asked.

"What you called me, 'little angel', that is what my father used to call me."

"Then it must true, Raquel. You must be an angel if the two of us to see it."

Her face looked less severe at this thought.

"Now", he said, "Take me to where this map shows the 'forearm'."

*　　*　　*

Reaching the spot indicated, Jackson held up the map. All the way, Raquel, had asked him what he was thinking about, but he did not want to say until he was certain. If he was correct, it could mean great deal to her and her dying little village.

He turned and paced off some steps away from the edge of the arroyo, checked the map, then turned slightly to his right, guessing as best he could from the position of the Sun, where West was. He paced some more. Then satisfied that he was at least in the area he was looking for, he got down on his hand and knees to dig in the dry dirt with his knife.

Raquel watched in silence for a full half hour, wondering all the while what this loco gringo was doing. She could not believe that she let such a man in her house, dying or not. Yes, he was handsome, and would be more so with some weight on him, but that was not a reason to follow one so easily fooled. That was why she had not followed her foolish father. Now, he seemed to have come back into her life in the form of this odd gringo. She could stand to watch no more.

"I am leaving. I hope you enjoy digging in the dirt like a dog, perhaps you will find a bone for your supper. You are just like my simple minded father."

"Wait, Raquel. I think I found it. Come quickly."

She hesitated, thinking it over. She had come this far on a fool's journey; would a few more moments with this man harm her any? She walked over to where he was working.

As she stood over him, using his knife, he traced the outline of what looked like buried adobe bricks set in a row. He continued to trace and dig as she looked on. Soon he came to a point where the bricks turned sharply as if in a building where the line came to—a wall. This must be remnants of some kind of structure! She had lived here all her life and had never seen it. How was it that Jackson had found it?

In answer to her unasked question, Jackson said, "I found this because it is here on the map."

"See?" he said as he traced his finger from one part of the map to the other.

Raquel looked back to the edge of the arroyo and then back to where they stood. Yes, the map did show Jackson where to look, but what is this map?

"It is a surveyors map, little angel. This looks like a building where maybe workers lived or stored their equipment. They must have planned to be here a long time if they put up a place like this. See the drawings that look like boxes?", Jackson said as he pointed them out on the map, "They look crude now, but that's only because the some of the lines have been worn down by age. This must be a real old document."

She gave him a questioning look, urging him to go on.

"It all came to me while you were telling me about the map. The words you translated stirred memories of a time when I was a kid. I remember I would hang around the local assayer's office making a pest of myself. Now and then I would even earn a penny for doing an odd job. Mostly, though, I used to sit in there and listen to great trails men tell stories of newfound lands. Some of them were trappers, living off the land, others were men called surveyors who worked for the Army. They always had the most interesting equipment, which I was never allowed to touch. I don't remember everything I heard there, but I do remember the word 'forearm' when they were talking about stream or somewhere that water ran. I thought it was funny—even scary—at the time. The more you translated, the more I remembered how the other words related to that one. One of them was 'meridian' which they told me had to do with finding where things are again after they found them the first time. Anyway, I remembered that the words on the map were all words used by these surveyors who'd go out and chart the land. Maybe the men who drew this map worked for the Mexican Army and that is why this is a 'federale document' as you called it?

What this means is that these places that are marked 'water' might be places to get water, they maybe locations of natural wells found by these men."

Raquel, looked doubtful, "But the water did flow once, what happened to it?"

"Let's take a walk and maybe we can find out. I have an idea."

Without waiting for an answer Jackson trotted back to the edge of the arroyo and began a descent into it. With just his head protruding over the bank, he turned and waited for Raquel, who did not seem like she wanted to follow him anymore. "Come on, little angel. You want to know, don't you? I won't let you get hurt."

She came to where he was and held out her hand so Jackson could help her down the side of the steep little ravine. When the came to the bottom, Jackson looked at the map and pointed to the base of a small hill some 500 yards from where they stood. Slowly, going through the overgrown brush while watching for rattle snakes and scorpions, they made their way to the foot of the hill.

Jackson immediately began pulling brush aside, tearing it out at its root when possible. "Careful now Raquel. Don't step anywhere unless you are sure there is ground under your feet."

Raquel chose to stand still and watch Jackson as he worked. She admired his earnestness but she was beginning to think she was correct—he is a crazy as her father was. Then he disappeared. He had sunk into the Earth itself!

Stepping gingerly to the spot where Jackson had stood, she saw his hand come up from what appeared to be a very deep hole. He had managed to grab some brush on his way down so he did not hit bottom. Now he used the brush as a rope to climb out of the pit.

"Dang, Raquel. I was right and darn near killed myself proving it." Brushing himself off, he took the map out of his shirt pocket.

Pointing he said, "See here? These spots marked 'water'? The two of them are at the base of this hill just where this hole is and most likely one other, so we have to be careful."

Jackson bent down and cut a long sapling. Stripping it down with his knife, he made a pole out of it. Now, walking slowly, he probed the low brush ahead of him. Finally, it disappeared half way into the ground. Jackson carefully cleared the brush around the edge of the second hole, while pointing it out to Raquel.

"But what does this mean?"

"Well a couple of things, I expect. These here two wells must have been the source of the stream water. The men must have dug the holes and just let the water flow, never expecting that some time, down the road, they would dry up, taking your stream and your town with it.

But this means that they may not have dug at the other well locations they marked on the map. Those wells would have been downstream and underwater. That means that we should be able to dig there and find water. Maybe water enough to get the town back on it's feet again. Let's go."

He took her hand and lead her slowly out of the immediate area, then quickly back to where they had started. With Raquel reading the map, he stepped off paces to where he thought a well might be. He figured that the surveyors might have marked them in some way since they made the effort to put them on the map; he remembered the men of his youth as being very particular and careful. After about a half dozen tries, he was ready to give up. Then he fell flat on his face. Getting up, dusting himself off, he looked at what tripped him. There beneath his feet, covered in low brush was a rock formation that looked a lot like an arrow.

"This is it, Raquel. This must be one of the well spots. Those rocks look too carefully placed to be accidental."

"Perhaps, Jackson. But why an arrow? Why not an X or something like that?"

"That I don't know, but I've got to dig here to see if we can find water. Lets go get some shovels."

Raquel was looking at the map, only half listening.

Now it was her turn to walk off without a word. But she was not walking off in anger, to Jackson's eye, she was pacing off steps. He stood and watched her lovely figure as she drew further away. He must be slipping, he was just now realizing what a remarkable body his sweet angel possessed. She was not a very tall angel, but her frame was hard and lean from working on her homestead. His mind was brimming in warm pleasant thoughts when he heard her call out.

Dashing to where she stood, he looked at where she was pointing. There was another arrow at her feet. "See mister kid surveyor, you are not the only one who can figure out maps." She said impishly.

Overwhelmed by her smoldering beauty and bright mind, Jackson scooped her up and kissed her hard on the lips. She kissed back, then pushed away smiling. "Wait Jackson. There is more to find. See, we have found four of the marked spots, the two holes and these two rock formations, but that means that there is one more. Lets follow the direction of the arrow, as I did. We should be able to find it."

He smiled at her cleverness as they went off and found the last spot. They piled more rocks on top of all the markers as they worked there way backwards to make them easier to find when they returned.

"Raquel, are there men who can still do a good day's work in the village?"

"Yes and they may help us if I talk to them."

"Great. If you can inspire some hope in them, they will join us. If not, I will dig the wells myself, but first I have to see something."

Climbing on top of the piled rocks, Jackson turned slowly in each direction, finally stopping and mumbling to himself. He seemed to be working on a puzzle.

"Okay Raquel, here is the plan," he said from atop the mound, "We go see the men, we ask them to help dig the wells. But first, we must build a dam!"

Jumping down, he took her hand and lead her back to the edge of the arroyo. All the while she was thinking about what kind of loco gringo would want to build a dam in the desert in a dry stream?

*   *   *

Raquel had asked the town Padre to ring the church bell to gather the people. Standing on the church steps she explained what she and Jackson had found. The reaction was a mixture of joy and suspicion as the villagers looked upon the dusty gringo stranger who showed up in their village just the day before.

Sensing their distrust, Raquel explained how Jackson had come to the town, how he had tried to help her father and how he almost died because of it. This softened the mood of the crowd somewhat, but there were still those who were cynical about the loss of the water. They were bitter and sure there was no more to be found. They would not work. This attitude seemed to grip the crowd even though their attitude toward Jackson had changed. Why dig in a dry river? Why build a dam in the middle of it. Jackson had still not explained this part to Raquel.

"Translate for me Raquel. I want to tell them why we need a dam."

She was startled—and secretly pleased—at his use of the word "we". So he now lived in Arroyo Seco? With who?

"The reason the first wells 'failed' is because the men let the water run off. They must have thought the wells would never dry up. So, they created a stream. We have to dam up one end of the arroyo and create a lake instead!"

Raquel, excited by his words, explained his idea enthusiastically to the crowd. They were not so enthusiastic, though some nodded in agreement with the idea of a dam. Jackson was upset at the lack of support he seemed to be getting. Raquel sensed this and admonished the crowd for their doubts. Still, they did not see any point in the effort.

Finally Raquel turned to Jackson, sadly, and said, "They will not help. They are too tired and sick of the arroyo to go near it. You have to understand, we have been dying very slowly. We do not want to look upon what is killing us."

"Fine then," replied Jackson angrily. "Tell them this. Tomorrow morning I will go to the arroyo, build the dam, and dig the wells by myself. When the water comes rising up out of the ground, saving their town, they can have it for free. I will leave it to them as I go." He stormed off.

As he left he could hear Raquel angrily reproaching the townspeople. Not that it would do any good.

*   *   *

The next morning he loaded up Stella—who was back in full health now—with a pick, shovel, a full canteen, and a lunch mama had prepared. Raquel had found some old bullets, that her father had, that fit in his gun just in case they came across a rattlesnake. He mounted Stella, Raquel climbed in the saddle behind him.

As they rode, he felt that he could have ridden on like this forever. Raquel rested her head gently on his shoulder, her arms around his waist. He barely felt her slight weight leaning on him, but he could feel the exciting curves of her body and the gentle strength in her arms. She would need this strength.

They searched "downstream", away from the hill, this time. Jackson was looking for the narrowest point across from bank to bank without getting too far down since he did not know how much water there would be when, and if, he found any. He did not share this last doubt with Raquel.

Once a likely spot was identified, they went to opposite sides of the arroyo and began to tumble rocks into it. Jackson had wanted Raquel to work with him, but she insisted on working one side alone stating, correctly, that the work would go faster. She was a wonderful young woman.

They worked on the dam for a week. Each day coming home dusty, scratched, and hungry. Mama, though doubtful about the operation, always had a hearty meal ready for them and a nice pile of hay for Stella.

Finally, Jackson was satisfied the dam would hold. He had cut some small saplings from the side of the hill and dragged them down the construction area. He mixed these in with the stones to give the work added support. He really wanted some mud to pack in the smaller holes, but that would have to wait for the water.

The next day, he began digging.

*   *   *

Now and then, as they had worked, town's people had come out to see what progress they had made. Grudgingly, according to Raquel, they said they admired the loco gringo for his sincerity if not for his intelligence. She enjoyed telling him this and giving him a quick hug afterward. They had not kissed anymore since their first one, though Jackson thought of doing this—and more—almost constantly.

Digging went slowly. The earth, hardened and baked by the unforgiving Sun, was not willing to let anyone incur on it without a fight. After a solid week, the hole was only about 10 feet deep. Jackson would dig and Raquel would haul the dirt out of the hole in a bucket with a rope on it. Though she was small, she had amazing stamina. Still, Jackson was getting frustrated. He had no idea how deep he had to go to find water, but he felt he should break through at anytime. The dirt had started to be more moist the last few days. As it grew moist, it was easier to dig, but heavier to haul out. He was afraid that his little angel was overdoing it. He thought about swapping jobs with her, but he would not be able to watch her go down into the whole if there were any chance of it caving in. If someone was going to die during this adventure, he wanted to be the one. By now he was not sure if he could have gone on living without Raquel by his side.

He filled the bucket once more and tugged on the rope, the signal telling her to pull it up. But this time, Raquel did not respond. Using his climbing rope, he pulled himself quickly out of the hole. Raquel was lying next to it, passed out. He wet his neckerchief and put it over her face while lying next to her in the dirt. She came around, but was too weak to talk. He picked her up and carried her to where Stella was grazing in the shade. He gently lifted her on first, then climbed on and rode as fast as he could while holding Raquel so she would not fall.

Mama came running out of the house at the sound of Stella's pounding hoofs. Jackson abruptly halted and slid off the saddle, Raquel in his arms. He immediately took her into her room and laid her gently on her bed. Mama, seeing the problem, made motions for him to leave, when he hesitated, she pantomimed that she would need to undress her daughter. Jackson waited in the kitchen.

A while later mama came out and, though he could not understand everything, she made motions indicating that Raquel would be all right, but she needed to rest. Then she pointed in the direction of the town and went into a tirade so animated, Jackson was glad that he could not understand her. She then grabbed her shawl and stormed out the door, apparently to go tell someone exactly what she had just said!

Jackson went into Raquel's room. She looked so beautiful and so peaceful, that he wanted to kiss her. But he would not disturb her. He was as angry as mama was at the townspeople, but he would use his anger in a different way. Making sure everything was secure, he mounted Stella and rode back to the arroyo to keep digging.

After an hour of shoveling, climbing out to pull up the bucket, then climbing back down, he knew that he could not keep up this pace, but he would not give up, he would never give up. If it meant getting Raquel her town back, he would dig until he died.

After his next descent, he heard noises—voices—coming from above. Looking up, he saw mama peering over the side of the hole, a couple of men were also looking down on him. One of them started to pull the bucket of dirt up. At first Jackson was going to stop him, but mama made a gesture like it was okay.

He climbed out to see what was going on. As he emerged from his hole, he saw what must have been most of the town's men standing along the edge of the arroyo, everyone had a pick, a shovel, or any other kind of digging tool they could find. They were all there to help.

Jackson waved everyone down. Using what little Spanish he knew combined with what little English some of the townspeople knew, he showed them the spots of the other two wells. Soon every man was digging or hauling dirt. For two days it went on like this. Children came out to watch them work and mothers brought baskets of food for the men.

The holes were getting dug more quickly now and soon the other two were almost as deep as the one he and Raquel had started. Still Jackson was getting frustrated. Where was the water? Had he misinterpreted the map, the holes at the base of the mountain and everything else involved in this folly?

On the third day, Raquel came out to the arroyo. She was still weak from dehydration, but she was able to sit under a small scrub tree on next to it and watch the work. Jackson spent every moment he was not digging sitting with her. They held hands as they watched the progress.

The next day was particularly disappointing. One wall had collapsed in another well nearly trapping one of the diggers. That well was now half as deep as it had been a few minutes before. This made all the town men angry. They threw down there shovels and began to leave. Jackson was fed up, too. The feeling of disappointment with the accident, the frustration of not finding water, and the nagging anger he had at himself for pushing Raquel so hard that she could have died was more than he could stand.

He shouted at the men's retreating backs, "If you are going to quit, then so am I. What do I care if your village dries up and blows away. You can have it, you can have all of it."

With that he sent his shovel, violently and with all his strength, sailing to the bottom of his and Raquel's well. As he turned to leave, he thought heard a rumbling behind him. Looking down into the well, he saw that the shovel had penetrated a foot or two into the ground. All around the shovel, water was coming up. Slowly at first, then in great gushes.

"Run", he shouted to everyone who was left in the arroyo, "Run as fast as you can." Then he ran himself.

Raquel, sensed a problem and began shouting at the men in Spanish exhorting them to run. They joined Jackson in his mad dash to the bank of the arroyo. Just as they all reached the top edge, a great spout of water came up out of the ground. It went up and up, finally breaking in the wind and showering down on everyone. It was as if a cloud had burst open just over their heads. Everyone shouted and cheered.

Jackson found Raquel and held her close to him, both were soaking wet and enjoying it. Mama was dancing to silent music with one of the men from the village.

As the spout wound down, the arroyo began to fill. The water spread quickly toward the makeshift dam Jackson and Raquel had built. He watched and held his breath as the water rose against it. It held. But the water continued to rise. Soon it was spilling over the edge of the dam. Jackson swore at first, then realized the water was leveling off. It looked like they would lose some of it, but in the mean time, the town would have a small water fall where they could go to get water. He immediately dubbed the sight Little Angel Falls.

Raquel was holding him tightly around the waist as she said, "My father was not a fool after all Jackson, and he did find gold. The only kind of gold that would save our town. We all owe him a great debt."

Jackson turned and kissed Raquel passionately. She did not pull away.

He looked up from the kiss, "I owe him more than anyone else, my beautiful little angel. He sent me on a journey where I discovered more treasure than any man could ever hope to find. I found you. I love you, Raquel."

Standing on her tip toes, she pulled him to her and kissed him, passionately, after a long moment, she said, "I love you too loco gringo Jackson."

Hearing their names called, they turned to look where mama was standing arm and arm with the Padre slightly tilting her head in the holy man's direction. They both laughed then took their first swim in Lake Aqua Dulce.

THE END

SAVING ABRAHAM

"You realize that it will not work, Johnson?" questioned Locke, "Not only that, it is a prohibited practice. You will never get a license from the Time Management Bureau."

Johnson did not pay attention to Locke's query, instead he remained stooped over his most recent treasure; the last known paper copy of Louis J. Weichmann's epic historical saga "A True History of the Assassination of Abraham Lincoln and the Conspiracy of 1865." He had just come into possession of the tome a week before and since then he had become totally absorbed by it. Moreover, impracticalities and permits were things that put Johnson off—he left these fiddling matters to his partner Locke.

"You know that if you take the voyage without permission, you will have your license for Time Travel revoked. Worse, if you disrupt what has already occurred, you may not have this future to return to!"

"What are you mumbling about now?" asked Johnson, "More worries about my upsetting what is by changing what was?"

"Yes, since you put it so lightly."

"Well stop worrying. We have not yet concluded that the present can be changed by altering the past, but if it can, then saving Abraham Lincoln from an assassin's bullet can only improve our lot."

"That is the point.", countered Locke, "You say 'our lot.' If you change the past, we may not have a 'lot' in the here and now. We may have never had a 'lot' anywhere!"

"Negative speculations, Locke? Where would we be now if we had listened to all of those negative speculations that surrounded our work? I will tell you. We would have never invented the Timatron, and time travel would still be a notion of science fiction writers the world over. Imagine that. The greatest invention of man; a machine that can not only move a person through the dimension of time but that of space as well, a machine that allows a lowly scientist like myself in Atlanta, year 2145, to visit the birth of Christ in Bethlehem, year 0000!. This machine would only be speculation if we listened to those who said we could not build it."

"But the council will—"

"Damn the council! There would be no council if it weren't for us!"

"Still, they are empowered to stop you."

"Nonsense, Locke. The government only empowers them to stop people who ask for their permission. I will not ask."

This last response so disturbed Locke that he began pacing the room—as he always did when agitated. Johnson watched his dear partner and felt bad that his ways of doing things upset his friend. Poor, Locke! A "by the book" man from cradle to grave! An invaluable asset to someone like Johnson whose head was always in the sphere of a separate reality and never in present corporeality.

Nevertheless, Johnson was going to continue with his mission.

"Oh, don't fret so, Locke", soothed Johnson, "I have thought it all out. I firmly believe that changing one event in the course of time cannot change the course forever. Time is! Time will always be!"

"And what does that mean?", shot back Locke.

"It means that I have drawn some conclusions from my recent studies concerning our visits to the time of the dinosaurs."

"The dinosaurs", cried Locke, "You wish to risk the present and future of humanity based on something that occurred hundreds of millions of years ago?"

"Calm down, Locke. I am not risking anything. If you give me a moment to go over my notes, I think you will agree with me."

Without waiting for assent, Johnson strode over to the Dataskimmer, punched in his access code, and searched for the subject "Dinosauria, The Death of".

Locke, in the meantime, knowing that there was no stopping Johnson when he began postulating on a new theory, made himself comfortable in the Easachair that he kept in the lab for these moments. He thought of the many times that he had sat in this very chair and listened to Johnson's rambling. Many times he had been able to glean a practical—and profitable—venture from his partner's meandering. The Timatron was just the latest of these enterprises. Well, he would listen to Johnson again, but if there seemed to be anything that would interfere with his leisure, Locke was going to be sure to stifle it. For if the truths be known, he did not care a great deal about humanity in general; but his own comfort in particular was something that he would not allow to be disturbed.

After a few nanoseconds of searching by the 'Skimmer and a few minutes of perusing of his notes, Johnson began: "Locke, you know that for centuries man speculated about how such a large, magnificent creature like the dinosaur had disappeared off the face of the Earth? We men blamed their demise on such diverse acts as comets striking the planet, mass plagues ravishing the ecosystems, drastic meteorological changes, etcetera, etcetera. Now, because of you, my friend, we now know that all of these theories were false."

"As will you recall, it was due to your suggestion that we made the first task of the Timatron a trip to see if any of these theories were true. This we did and we not only found that all of these theories were erroneous, we also found that man and the dinosaur existed at the same time. In one trip in time we put to rest two ideas that until then had been taken as fact!"

Johnson stopped to scan a note, make a slight change, then went on, "Therefore, in essence, Locke, we 'changed history'. What we thought had transpired had not happened at all! Instead, we found that it was man who had caused the demise of the dinosaurs. We infected them with bacteria that thrived in our bodies but was deadly to their kind. Our belief that both dinosaurs and men had existed in different times was merely due to our incompetent dating techniques. We were relying on the belief that dinosaurs and humans were made up of the same basic chemistry, which they are not. We discovered all of this yet the 'here and now', as you call it, remains unchanged."

"You're splitting hairs now, Johnson." rebutted Locke, "Your just manipulating words to justify playing God with man's future. No matter what we perceived the truth to be, the real events happened just so. These events were building blocks in the wall of the future. By discovering that the blocks may not have been formulated from the material we presumed they were made of, we did not change the blocks, we just painted them a different color. The blocks themselves remain."

"Ah, my good friend, Locke. Always the solid upright type, just as your imaginary wall is."

"Imaginary!"

"I apologize for the use of that word, Locke. It was a poor choice as you are a good man—who possesses or little no imagination. Your 'theory', as I will refer to it from now on, is based on the supposition that time is a fixed structure and that any movement of the structure would cause cracks in it, indeed, an earthquake in time would cause it to all fall down. I, for one, Locke, do not hold to this theory.

"Since you feel that I am lacking your insight, perhaps you will enlighten me with your beacon of intelligence." retorted a sarcastic Locke.

"I will, but not because I perceive you as being dimwitted, I just oppose your most concrete theory. I hope that you took no offense in my doubting you?"

"No, no." said Locke, "We have had differences before with no offense taken. None will be forthcoming at this time as well. Do continue."

"Very well, Locke.", Johnson replied.

He paused again for a time, gathering his thoughts before proceeding." In my mind I do not envision time as the unalterable edifice as you do. No, I see time as a river. A mighty river, one such as we have never seen in a physical presence on this or any other planet. Thus, I submit this parable: I am but a young boy, small in stature, standing on the banks of this mighty river. I am in awe of the greatness it presents to me. As if to exert some proximity of control over it, I reach my diminutive hand down to grasp a pebble. With a vigorous heave, I throw it into the river. Just for an instant, the river parts as my pebble breaks the surface. For a few seconds afterwards, ripples disrupt the flow, then the current quickly swallows them up as the river resumes its true course. In my theory, this true course represents the events in time that have already happened. Just like the mighty river running its course, the events will continue to occur regardless of any minor disruptions. At the most, all will be as it was with only minor shadings put on the events. What was good, may be better, what was bad may be worse. My saving Abraham Lincoln from an assassin's bullet, will be the first good rock."

Locke contemplated this idea. In all the years he and Johnson had been partners, he had never know this man to put any idea into words unless he had a great deal of certainty behind it. Could what he be saying now be true? If it was, could there be any financial gain for the firm of Johnson & Locke in it? His continued silence brought a response from Johnson.

"I know what you are thinking, Locke. You being the pragmatic person that you are, you are looking for a monetary gain if my concept is accurate. Is that true?"

"Someone has to look after the books, Johnson."

"And a fine job of it you do, Locke. If not for your rapacious side, I dare say we would not be in the position that we now occupy, but in this case, I have anticipated you."

"How so?" questioned a suddenly more attentive Locke.

"If my theory proves accurate, we will be able hire our services out to any person, and there will be plenty of them, who wishes to change the course of their family history or who simply wish to unburden themselves of a skeleton in their closet by changing one simple deed or the other. Who among us have not said 'If only I had done this differently.'? None would be my guess.

We could go back and change this item or that to suit the individual. The fees for our service would be one to fit the job. I speculate that none will be less than a king's ransom. What do you think?"

Locke became caught up in the last portion of his friend's speech. He was sampling the population of the planet for those rich enough to afford such an operation. By the time it he multiplied the amount by the fee, he had become bogged down in carry forwards ad infinitum! There were too many zeros! Just the way he liked it. Then a thought came to him that halted the calculations.

"Are you not forgetting one thing, Johnson?"

"What is that, Locke?"

"The Chaos Theory."

"Oh yes, 'chaos'. That was quite a popular little theory in the latter part of the 20th century was it not?. The 'if a butterfly bats it's wings in Tokyo, it will change the weather in Montana' group. Whatever became of them? I understand that the last of their leaders were jailed some time ago."

"Yes, yes, in the last Great Intellect Purge they were incarcerated for a time, but they were all released as being harmless fanatics."

"Well I surmise that says that about them." sniffed Johnson.

"I remember when the scientific community thought of us as being considered fanatics, too Mr. Johnson. If we had not come up with the Timatron, we may have well joined them behind bars."

"True." responded Johnson, "But we did, and we invented it using sound, acknowledged principles. Not unsound conjectures such as theirs."

"Johnson, you know as well as I do that all sound, acknowledged theories start out as unsound conjectures. You have to ask yourself "What if they are right?". What if the ripple caused by your rock manufactures a wave in time? What then?"

"Then we will know that they were right."

"You are willing to risk that?"

"At the minimal chance that a wave will occur balanced against our—and mankind's—possible gain, yes I am." concluded Johnson.

Locke sat quietly in his Easachair. Figures with many zeros after them spun through his head again. He pondered the practical and dubious points of both his argument and that of Johnson's. Both had merit, despite Johnson's snobbery regarding another group's theory. In Johnson's favor, they could make a sizable profit; those zeros were not too numerous to be ignored! On the other hand . . . .

"Okay Johnson. We will do it your way one time and hope that there will be another time to try again, but I promise you that if you destroy my future, I will come back as a ghost to haunt you. That is if I have a life in the first place."

This grisly approval satisfied Johnson, but he could tell that Locke still wondered about something. So he inquired: "What is it Locke? Do you need more assurances? If so, I have no more to give."

"No, Johnson, those that you have provided are quite good enough for me. But I do have one more question. Why Lincoln? Why not Kennedy, Sadat,

King, Gandhi or any of hundreds of other great men who have met their ends by the means of an assassin's bullet?"

Johnson squirmed while looking at his colleague, evidently he was trying to make a decision on a troublesome matter. With an unseen shrug, he appeared to have resolved the question, but he still did not answer right away. He walked over to Weichmann's book, picked it up, turned to a picture—the last photograph taken of Lincoln before he was killed—and looked at it quietly for some time. Locke began pacing again in hopes of getting his stubborn friend to come forward with an answer.

"For pity's sake stop pacing, Locke, I will tell you what you desire to know, but it is rather embarrassing as I have never held any secrets from you in the past. The fact is that I made a trip in the Timatron while you were in Washington DC securing the patents for it. I was curious about my lineage so I followed my ancestry back several generations. In doing so, I discovered, to my great discomfort, that my family had roots in the slave trade.

Roots! Ha! Much more than that! I discovered, and I would never reveal this to anyone else, that one of my greater-grandparents was a ruthless slave trader! As ruthless a one as there ever was. To him a black person was a machine. He used the women for his carnal pleasures—he bore many bastards by them—and he used the men for work. When the machines broke down or acted up, he would whip them—often to their death!

Yes, Locke. As I said, all families have skeletons, and I have found my own. In the first trip of our new venture, I will attempt to rid my family of the one we possess. By saving Lincoln, I believe I will greatly advance the rights of the black people and perhaps undo some of the damage perpetrated by my distant progenitor. If unsuccessful, I will know that I have at least tried."

*   *   *

Johnson sat strapped in the Timatron. Much preparation had taken place since Locke and he had agreed to go forward with the Lincoln project.

With the help of Weichmann's book, they decided to start the assignment shortly before dawn on April 7, 1865, one week before Lincoln died at Booth's hand. Johnson would arrive late at night, under the cover of darkness, on the outskirts of Georgetown near the banks of the Potomac River. He would arrive fully dressed and documented in the guise of a traveling liquor salesman—a man welcomed heartily by all, without question, in those wild times as long as his samples held out. He would also be a man that people expected be well funded. That is why Johnson was taking along $10,000 in greenbacks that Locke had purchased from several private collections. He needed this money just in case he had to buy his way into or out of any given situation.

For the night of April 14th, Johnson had a uniform from the Union army and fake facial hair in his bag. He and Locke had decided that the best way to have freedom of movement in and around Ford's Theater on that night was to pretend to be a part of the large army attachment that was kept in Washington to protect it from attack. Though fully documented as a soldier, Johnson expected no trouble, as there were few people who would challenge him. That an actor had found Lincoln so easily accessible to deliver a bullet to was grim testimony to this.

The only weaponry he would take was the necessary sidearm that men of that time carried. Locke had the idea of just eliminating Booth with a Vapor Ray, but Johnson had objected to this idea. For one, he was far from the assassin type; he was not sure that he could kill a man in cold blood no matter what end result was achieved by doing so. Finally, he wanted Booth caught and jailed for the crime he had planned to commit. It was important to Johnson that Booth be held accountable for plotting this evil deed.

Upon arrival in 1865, he would send the Timatron back to Locke with it programmed to return to him on his command. Although the Timatron was a small device, not much larger than ancient phone booths, hiding it in 1865 would be out of the question. If someone found it and damaged it, Johnson would be stranded in that era until Locke built or borrowed one in order to retrieve him.

Johnson planned to buy a horse or, better yet, due to his fragile posterior, a carriage and a team of horses. With this means of transport he would make his way to Washington where he planned to take a room in a boardinghouse near that of Mary E. Surratt, the mother of conspirator John H. Surratt, and the place where Weichmann stayed for several months before the assassination. From his position, Weichmann had been able to observe, quite oblivious of their intentions, the comings and goings of all the confederates involved in the plot to kill Lincoln. Johnson wanted this same view.

He needed to keep a close watch on the movements of Booth. If he was going to stop him as he planned he needed to be near him at the exact moment Booth intended to murder Lincoln. Just exposing his plot in some way to the authorities would not be enough for Weichmann showed in his book that the conspiracy was beginning to unravel in the weeks before it took place. The authorities had been aware that some sort of conspiracy was afoot, as they had made some preliminary investigations into the whereabouts of a few members the group. Johnson wanted the authorities to catch Booth with the gun in his hand.

To this end, Johnson also packed a number of portable Auditory Intensifying Devices, popularly known as "ears". These small, metal, numbered, button-like devices allowed a person equipped with the proper Auditory Implant Receptor to hear the conversations, even whispered conversations, of everyone within 35 feet of the device. Johnson had Locke place his receptor just under the lobe of his left ear so all he needed to do to activate it was to give the lobe a slight tug. With the portable "ear map", Johnson would be able to keep track of each place that he planted the ears.

Everything was ready. Johnson checked the destination coordinates one last time, gave a "thumbs up" to Locke who was standing by with his protective eye-wear on, and pressed the "GO" button on the control pad.

In an instant, the lab vanished into a swirling vortex of transmutating colors. Gold became red, red became purple, purple became pink, pink became gold as the cycle repeated itself. It was the same patterns every trip.

The slight disorientation that this always caused passed quickly. Johnson could see the years passing like seconds on the digital display panel in front of him. From past trips he knew that it would only be a matter of minutes before he arrived at the predestined time and place, still he marveled at the speed and precision of the machine that he had built with his own hands. As he passed through the 19th century, he checked his seat belt and prepared for what may be a rough arrival.

With a lurch, he was there. 1865! Immediately, Johnson knew that something was not right; the Timatron was still moving though the vortex had vanished. He could feel it steadily slipping to the right! He unbuckled his seat belt and jumped out just as the machine slid sideways two more feet. To his amazement, Johnson found himself knee deep in water. So that was the problem; over the centuries the Potomac had evidently changed its course. Now instead of being 20 feet into the woods as planned, the machine was teetering on the river's bank.

Johnson tried to push it further up onto the bank, but the muddy river bottom did not allow his boots to find any purchase. He scrambled onto dry land to try to right the time vehicle from that side only to find it leaning so precariously that he feared it would tip it into the river if he touched it. His only chance to save it was to send in back to Locke. As he opened the door of the Timatron and removed his pack the sudden loss of ballast caused the machine to begin sliding again. Johnson knew that this time it would not stop. At the last second, before the machine hit the water, Johnson pushed the "SEND" button on his remote control apparatus, returning the Timatron to his own time in an explosion of yellow light!

Johnson recoiled as searing pain overwhelmed his vision; he had forgotten how bright the flash from the Timatron was when it embarked on a journey. The haste required by the moment prevented him from preparing for it anyway. He fell back onto the damp grass, waiting for his eyes to regain their function.

This took some time, as it was so dark out that at first he was not sure if he had regained full use of his eyes. By feeling his way in the inky night, he managed to find an IllumaBall in his pack. This was a palm size device that emitted light when touching the skin; Johnson could quickly mute its light if necessary by simply closing his hand.

With this light, he went in search of the main rood. After a few futile attempts, he found one that appeared to lead in the direction of Georgetown. Checking his compass, he set off in what he felt would be the right direction.

An hour later there was still no sign of a town, though Johnson suspected he had passed some farms from the caterwauling of dogs at their post. The sun had started to rise, allowing Johnson to pocket the Illumaball. Another half-hour of walking brought him to the first building that he had seen in 1865. The decay of the outside of it made Johnson think that it was abandoned, but as he drew closer, he heard the sound of metal striking metal. In the ever-growing light, he was also able to see wisps of smoke coming from a crude hole in the roof. Whoever was inside did not hear Johnson approaching, as no one came out to greet him. So, he walked up to the large door, opened it, and let himself inside.

It was darker in the interior of the building than it was outside since the only illumination was the light from a forge that was tended by a dwarf. Stooped over an anvil stood a gnarled old man with glistening white hair and a fire singed beard to match, he was in the act of meticulously shaping what looked like an old fashioned andiron.

Johnson looked around and thanked his luck. He recognized this place now from the crude appointments as being a blacksmith shop; a perfect place for him to attain transportation if he were to find any.

Right now both men seemed so absorbed in their work that they took no notice of Johnson. He was about to say something to get there attention when the white-haired man spoke up.

"Well are you gonna stand there with the darned door open all day, or are you gonna come in?"

Johnson was so startled by this sudden recognition, that he almost slammed the door in his haste to close it. He took a breath and replied, "Why thank you for your kindness, my good man."

This response caused the old man to stop what he was doing and look at him. The dwarf showed no interest as he continued to stoke the furnace until the old man waved at him to desist. The man examined Johnson, apparently now curious about his visitor.

"Are you a preacher man?" he asked eyeing Johnson warily.

"Why no.", responded Johnson, "Why do you ask?"

"Because your a well-spoken young fella and I would rather you be a preacher than one of those damned southern dandies. You ain't a southerner are ya?"

Technically, he was, but that was 280 years into the future, for now he felt he should deny it. "Why no. I'm not."

"No? Well, I can hardly believe it, but it ain't my way to call a man a liar. Won't do to start now. What's it your doing out on the road this time of the mornin'?"

Johnson came prepared for this question. "My horse drew up lame a few miles back. I turned it loose and struck out on foot."

"Oh? So where you headed?"

"Into Georgetown first. I am going to call on a few saloons there to see if they are interested in my company's' line of alcoholic beverages. From there I am going on to Washington DC."

This information caused the old man's eyes to brighten; just as Johnson hoped they would.

"You ain't plannin' to walk the whole way are ya?"

"No replied Johnson, I was hoping to purchase a horse and if possible a carriage somewhere along the way."

"In that case it was durn lucky you happened onta me and my place. Durn lucky. I'm the only blacksmith between here an' Georgetown, an' I just happen ta have a rig for sale—but the price ain't cheap."

"How much are you asking for it?"

"Well it ain't mine ta begin with. It belongs ta old man Keenly just down the road a bit. He told me ta sell it fer whatever I can get fer it." The smithy stopped to ponder Johnson as if he was trying to calculate exactly how much money he had in his pockets. "I'd say $35.00 would be enough for Keenly. The rig isn't in the best of shape, but its ride able and it will get you where your going. The horse is worth more."

"All right sir, I will glad to pay you that much, I will take your word as a man of the road that the cost is equal to the value."

"Yeah, you sure are a rightly speakin' young man. You sure you ain't a preacher?"

"Quite sure my good man. As a matter of fact, I would consider it an honor if I could leave you a small sample of my whiskey products. If you like it, I would appreciate you telling any customers passing this way that the drink will be available in Georgetown soon. I am confident that I will be able to sell some to the local drinking houses."

"I'll go for that. Matter of fact, I'll take the whiskey as commission on my sale. Old Keenly don't drink no how."

Johnson could tell that this last statement was not truthful, but he did not care. This interaction with the blacksmith was just the type he needed to establish himself as the traveling liquor salesman that he was pretending to be.

*   *   *

In his lifetime, Johnson had never actually been in the presence of a horse, so when he saw the one he had just purchased, the size and statuesque beauty of the beast impressed him. Its hair was coal black with the only exception being a trace of gray in its long flowing main. He thought how criminal it was to use this elegant beast for such menial labor like pulling a buggy. Yet when the blacksmith proceeded to fit the animal to into its reigns, it appeared to delight in it. The animal sensed that it would soon be free of the confines of its corral. It wanted to run.

"Like I told ya, the durn horse is worth more than the rig. Durned if I know where Keenly got 'im, but I get the feeling that it belonged to one of those refined Confederate officers. What happened to the officer, I don't know— but with Keenly, I could guess."

Johnson did not want to think about this. He paid off the blacksmith, including his two bottles of "commission", and bid him ado. Getting the animal to move forward took a bit of practice on his part, but Johnson had studied videos on the Dataskimmer on how to do this. So, after a few aborted attempts, that caused the blacksmith to look at him rather curiously, he flicked the reigns just in a way the beast recognized and it moved towards the road. Once there, the intelligent animal seemed to know that he was to stay on the beaten down path for no matter how the road twisted and turned, the animal did not stray from it.

It was fortunate for Johnson that the road to Georgetown did not cross any major intersection. This way he did not have to remember to do anything more than to let the horse lead him on.

Johnson thrilled at the feel of transporting from one place to the other in such a fashion. He had never breathed air as clean as such there was on this crisp Spring morning. The cool fresh air running through his thinning hair was an experience that he soon decided was as close to pure ecstasy that any man would ever get.

These sensations made his arrival to the outskirts of Georgetown a bit of a disappointment but he had to refocus himself. He was in 1865 on a mission, not on a pleasure trip, though he vowed to come back to this time later with Locke so his dear friend could also experience this ecstasy.

It didn't take him long to find a saloon as he estimated that there was one on every other corner. After going through the charade of taking orders from three of these establishments, he chose to press on to Washington DC before nightfall prohibited him from traveling.

The road to Washington DC was so well traveled in this time that Johnson had no difficulty in finding his way there either and by the time he arrived, dusk was approaching. Johnson was proud of how proficient he had become at directing his horse. It turned out that he needed these skills due to the enormous bustle of activity in the young nation's capital. As he entered the city, he had to constantly watch for people and men on horseback who dashed out, apparently without care, in front of his rig. With some difficulty and with the aid of the proprietor of a dry goods store, Johnson found his way to his target location: Howard's Livery Stable, the same stable where, according to Weichmann, Booth often kept his horses.

Even more important than this fact was that the livery was located directly behind the Surratt boarding house, the very same place that Weichmann had lived with many of the 1865 conspirators. Johnson had no hope of getting a room there, but he did want to be nearby. His plan was to strike up a friendship with one of the Surratt boarders and wrangle and invitation into the house where he could then plant his "ears". He would have to work quickly, but he felt he could accomplish this.

By the time Johnson had paid for the boarding of his horse, the city's lamp lights were being lit, making it urgent that he find a place to stay for at least one night before launching his plan. As luck would have it, the neighborhood was full of boarding houses including one located directly across the street from the Surratt house.

Johnson's knock on the front door of this establishment was answered by a petite young lady who was probably much older than she looked. Behind her, in the room, Johnson could see that she had a guest. To his query about a room for the night, she said she was sorry but no rooms were available at this time. She began to give him the names of a few other establishments in the area that might be able to accommodate him when her guest spoke up.

"I can put him up at my place, Anna. That is if he is not too fussy."

Looking up, Johnson saw a short, squat, and very homely, woman approach the door.

"Are you sure Mary. I thought your house was full."

"Like I said, as long as he isn't to fussy, I can put him up. All the rooms are full, but I have nice dry attic with a cot in it that he can have if he don't mind cleaning it out a bit."

Johnson stood by dumbly listening to this; he knew who this lady was. Mary! She owns a boarding house! This lady could only be Mrs. Mary Surratt— and she was offering him lodging!

"Well you going to speak or are you going to stand there with your mouth open all night. If you don't want the bed, I can sure find someone else to fill it. This town has been overrun with people since the war started winding down." Johnson came out of his haze. "Oh no ma'am, I would gladly accept lodging in your home. I am sure that it is a nice one and that your attic is very comfortable indeed."

"Well, another well-spoken man! You haven't been studying to be a priest like my young Mr. Weichmann have you? If so, I don't want you. I got enough people making me feel guilty about things as it is, I don't need no more men of the cloth doing so."

Johnson could barely contain himself in the presence of this mannish little troll. Weichmann had often said in his book that he was sure Mrs. Surratt knew about the conspiracy all along even though she espoused her innocence right up to the time the hang man put the noose around her neck. This last comment made Johnson sure that Weichmann had been correct in his assumptions. Guilty conscience indeed!

"Quite to the contrary." Johnson finally replied, "In fact I am a traveling spirits salesman. I would be happy if you would do me the honor of sampling some of my wares. It is a great tonic for guilty consciences."

Mrs. Surratt glared harshly at Johnson. She was clearly upset at this remark, but her apparent greed won out. "You just never mind my conscience young man. It will take care of itself. Now pick up your bags and let's get across the street before the day's light is gone entirely. It isn't safe to out after dark in these wild times."

*   *   *

Johnson was thankful that he did not meet any of the other boarders as Mrs. Surratt showed him to his attic room. Along the way she was kind enough to point out the rooms of the other boarders. In particular interest was the one she said was occupied from time to time by "a young actor". Of course this actor had to be John Wilkes Booth the man who assassinated Lincoln and Johnson's target. Just before going up the stairs to the attic room, Mrs. Surratt opened a small closet door. Out of it she took a broom that she handed to Johnson. "You will be needing this." she said.

Indeed he did. The attic room was dry, but it was very dusty. With the aid of the broom, a bucket of water, and some rags Johnson was able to carve out a small clean zone where he could live and operate for the next week. Mrs. Surratt told him the meal times and said he was welcome to join the other guests if he wished but that no one would wait for him. This was fine since

Johnson planned to avoid direct contact with all of the other lodgers as much as possible. He offered the excuse to Mrs. Surratt that he usually took meals in the establishments he sold to, so he would most likely not be present at meals.

The next two days were uneventful, but busy, days for Johnson as he managed to avoid all the other tenants of the house. He soon discovered a small balcony outside of an upstairs parlor that was located at the rear of the house. There was a rickety, but usable, set of stairs leading up to it. It was from these stairs that he was able to get in and out of the house without notice. During this two-day period, Johnson also managed to place "ears" in every room of the house. Then while sitting in his attic room he was able to listen to every word spoken by anyone in the house. To his disappointment, nothing was directly said concerning the conspiracy to assassinate Lincoln.

Johnson knew that on April 10th, Booth would be in the Surratt house. An excerpt from Weichmann's book mentioned that Booth and several others would meet in the downstairs parlor to share a letter from Mrs. Surratt's son, John, who was in New York. That day, while everyone was out, Johnson placed two more ears in this room. He wanted to make sure that every word spoken was recorded.

For the most part, the conversation went as reported, only filled out with the usual banter between long-time associates. One thing Johnson observed that Weichmann had not mentioned was that Booth seemed to be very irritable. Johnson heard a man pacing heavily to and fro in the room. From the conversation, Johnson deduced that the footsteps belonged to Booth. He seemed to be very anxious. His words were delivered in a terse, rough edged manner, had he not been among friends, Johnson thought he might have sworn on a few occasions. At one point Booth asked one of the ladies present (Weichmann reported this woman to be a certain Miss Ward) for the address of "that lady" again. Johnson heard the sound of a piece of paper being handed to Booth who had tramped over to Miss Ward. After holding it for less than a minute, Booth returned to paper to her, then went to the corner of the room.

A period of silence was followed by the sound of footsteps as people left the room with no one saying anything more to Booth. After a few minutes a man spoke. This had to be Weichmann. He had reported that at this time he talked to Booth concerning the end of the Confederacy. Booth reacted angrily to this by lecturing Weichmann on how the final remnants of the Confederate army could take to the mountains for a last stand of resistance. Weichmann listened politely until Booth was finished, then excused himself for the night.

That left only Booth in the room. For a time he paced some back and forth mumbling to himself. The sound of his boots on the floor prevented Johnson from clearly hearing Booth's words, but it was quite evident to him that the man in some kind of very deep anguish. Finally, Johnson heard him stride over to window and pull the drapes fully closed. He then sat down heavily still mumbling. Johnson picked up the gain on all the ears in the room, so that Booth's mumbling would be clear to him.

"... . You are mine Mary, mine! Not his! Not his!" With that Booth explosively ran out of the room.

Johnson heard his footsteps race down the stairs and out the front door.

The coming night brought little sleep for Johnson as his mind buzzed with the mystery that Booth's words had created. In all the writings of Weichmann, the only "Mary" mentioned was Mrs. Surratt. Could it be that Booth was in love with her? This seemed unlikely not only because of their age differences, but also because Booth was a very well known handsome actor; he could have most any woman he wished. So why would he pursue Mrs. Surratt? As well as this, Booth's Mary was apparently involved with another man. Mrs. Surratt, as far as Johnson could tell, was not.

With these puzzles swirling in his mind, Johnson drifted off into a fitful sleep.

*   *   *

The next day as Johnson returned from getting his dinner, he was surprised to find someone in the back parlor. He had become caught up in the revelry that surrounded Washington DC that day since General Robert E. Lee, the leader of the confederate forces had surrendered to General Ulysses S. Grant the night before. Celebrations were taking place in every quarter of the town as a weary nation realized that the Civil War had finally ended. This atmosphere of triumph and gaiety had made him incautious when he entered the boardinghouse. Normally he would have looked through the window to see if anyone was in the room but this time he did not. So when he entered the room only to find it occupied, he was taken aback.

As he came through the door, a slightly built, mustachioed man turned from the book he was reading.

"I beg you pardon, sir." stammered a flustered Johnson, "I did not intend to disturb your reading."

"No? Then what did you intend to do coming in the back way like this?" the man asked accusingly.

"Nothing nefarious for sure my good man." replied Johnson, feigning indignation, "I was just going up to my attic room."

"Ahhh. Then you must be Mr. Johnson, the new boarder that Mrs. Surratt informed us of."

"I am indeed one and the same."

"We, all of our fellow boarders that is, were beginning to wonder if you were real or just a figure of Mrs. Surratt's invention. Now I understand why we have not seen you about. The rest of us use the front door for our comings and goings."

"As would I if my comings and goings were not in the quantity as they are. Also since on many of these occasions I do not get in till quite late at night, I chose to use this entrance to save the rest of the boarders from any unnecessary disturbances."

"Well, Mrs. Surratt told us that you seemed to be a kindly man. I now believe this to be true, and I for one thank you for thinking of us."

"In return, I thank you for not taking offense at my disturbing you now. So, if you would excuse me, I would like to go up and get the dust of the day off of me."

"By all means, sir. If you find yourself in need of anything, feel free to come to my room, just at the end of this hallway."

"This hallway?"

"Why yes. Why do you look so startled by this?"

"Then you must me Mr. Weichmann?"

"Yes I am, does this mean something to you?"

Johnson's mind was racing, "No, nothing at all really. It is just that Mrs. Surratt spoke highly of you and I hoped that I would meet you.", he lied.

"Then your hopes have been fulfilled. I pray you are not disappointed."

"Not at all. It is an honor to meet you.", Johnson replied in all sincerity. "I will be only too glad to call on you if I need anything."

"See that you do Mr. Johnson. I always appreciate company."

As Johnson strode off to his room he wondered if he had somehow tossed another stone into the river of time. For in Weichmann's writing, no mention was made of a boarder named Mr. Johnson, although every other one of them was described in great detail.

The answer had to be that he was not mentioned because he was not "there" during the period of time covered by the book. He had only arrived in 1865 four days earlier. He wondered now if he would be in the book when he returned to 2145?

*   *   *

For most of the next two days nothing eventful occurred. Johnson had been so shaken by his encounter with Weichmann, that he was now extra careful to avoid any contact with the other boarders. Listening through the hidden ears revealed nothing more, nothing to hint that a conspiracy was about. This lead Johnson to wonder if Weichmann was truthful in his account of these days or if he was just a man with a case of over-active imagination. Yet many of the things Weichmann reported had come to pass. Johnson could only conclude that the conspiracy, if there was one, was now so set in place that no further planning was needed.

It was very late on the eve of the assassination when the soft humming of the alarm on his "ear map" woke him from a light sleep. Someone was speaking in one of the rooms. The room was the one that Booth stayed in while in residence in the house. Johnson tugged on his ear lobe.

"Mary—"

"No John, do not call me that here. I must continue to be 'Mrs. Slater' when I am in this place. If anyone were to discover that I came here, I do not know what he would do."

Johnson sat up straight. Mrs. Slater? This Mary woman he had heard Booth mumbling about was the mysterious Mrs. Slater? She is a woman Weichmann spoke of in his book. A woman whose whereabouts had never been discovered during the investigation following the assassination. It seems she had, as Weichmann so eloquently put it, "passed into the future as one of the mysteries of the Surratt house".

To Weichmann's knowledge this woman had visited the house twice, but he did not mention her on this night of all nights. Johnson could only assume that Weichmann was not aware of her presence. He thought of how ironic it was that Weichmann's mystery woman and Johnson's mystery woman were actually one and the same. To Weichmann's credit, clever man that he was, he had suspected that "Mrs. Slater" was a fraudulent identity. Johnson wished that he could tell Weichmann that he was right.

"Damnation!", Booth swore, "I have had enough of this pretending. Must I continue my profession into my real life forever? No! It is time to let the world know our secret. I want to go out and shout my love for you so that all will here."

"But you mustn't, not yet. The time is not right."

"The time may never be right as you see it! We should have come right out and spoke of our love the night we met in Meadville. I loved you immediately and I know that you loved me as well. You could not have acted as you did purely out of lust alone."

"Yes that night, that insane night. You poor man, you almost incriminated yourself that night."

"You know that what I wrote was written in a strictly metaphorical sense. I only planned to kidnap not kill. I have not the nerve to kill a man."

"I know that John, but few others do, and just the threat of such an action can get you put in jail in these times."

"I am not afraid of jail. I am not afraid of anything if you would only be mine in public as well as in private."

"You are a brave man, John. You are too good for me, I know this."

"No Mary, no. That is just an image of yourself that he has put in your mind. You are kind, beautiful, and gentle. You must not feel inferior in anyway to him or to me."

"Oh John. Oh John. I love you. That is why seeing you tonight is so difficult, for I must not see you again. We must end this tonight."

"Never! Never!" Booth shouted.

"Quiet my dear! You will awaken Mr. Weichmann."

"Weichmann! That meddling fool! Always sneaking about seeing and hearing things that he should not."

"Yes, Weichmann. I fear him. I dread that he knows more about your past plans than he lets on. I think that he will go to his superiors in the War Department with his suspicions. If he were to do so an investigation of you would surely lead them to me. That is why we must end this now. But fear not dear John, I will come back to you when I know it is time."

"When will that be? When I am too old to enjoy your company? And what is to say that the years will no make you feel differently about me? You may never wish to return to me."

Johnson heard the woman go to Booth, they seemed to embrace. "Never fear that John. I will always love you."

"Than you must not leave me."

"I must."

"I will not let you, Mary. I will not allow him to have you if I cannot."

"You frighten me when you speak so John. I know that you do not mean it, but it frightens me still."

"But I do mean it now, Mary. I cannot live without you."

"Oh dear John, lets not talk of that any more. I have arranged for us to have one more night together, let us take full advantage of it as if it has to last us a lifetime."

"Ah yes, a lifetime. But who decides how long that is?"

With that Johnson tugged on his earlobe, shutting off his listening device— after all he was not a voyeur. He was a scientist on a mission, a mission that became more baffling by the minute.

Who was this Mary known as "Mrs. Slater"? What did she mean when she when she referred to Booth's "past mission"? Does this mean he has given up his plan to kill Lincoln? Is that why there had been no talk of it in the house?

Then again, what did Booth mean when he said he did not have the nerve to kill a man? Did this mean that another man and not he had carried out the assassination? For surely Lincoln was murdered. If this was the case, should he look for another suspect at this late date? Should he go back to 2145 and start over? What was it about the town of Meadville that sounded so familiar to Johnson?

Johnson forced himself into another fitful sleep that night despite having all these new questions facing him. He knew that he would need all his strength if he were to succeed in his mission the next day. What ever that mission turned out to be.

*   *   *

Johnson's heart pounded so hard that he could feel the beating of it in his chest. He was crouched behind a large partition in President Lincoln's box; it was in the box just as Weichmann had reported it would be. All Johnson had to do was to move it slightly so he would be completely hidden while still being comfortable as he waited for the key players in this drama to arrive. In the back of his mind a nagging thought made him wonder who those players would be.

He started the day by changing in to his Union Army soldier disguise. His plan was to loosely follow Booth's trail; a task made easier by the information provided in Weichmann's book as it told exactly where Booth had been during different parts of the day. According to this information, Booth was due to arrive back at the Surratt house sometime after 10:00 a.m.

Johnson had stayed in his room until just before that time. His trailing of Booth would start when Booth left the house.

While he waited for him to arrive, Johnson had recalled why Meadville sounded familiar to him. According to Weichmann, Booth had given a one-night performance in that town in August of the previous year. Nothing immediately remarkable came from this except for something that was discovered in his hotel room after the actor had checked out. This discovery was an inscription that was found on one windowpane, it read: "ABE LINCOLN departed this life August 13th, 1864, by the effects of poison.". It was only later, after the assassination, that the handwriting on the window and Booth's handwriting were compared. They were identical. Weichmann noted this incident citing it as the first time anyone knew of hostile feelings by Booth towards the President. How this information fit into the puzzle, Johnson had not been able to ascertain before he had to leave the house.

For the rest of the day, Johnson shadowed Booth. He was standing outside Ford's Theater when Booth spoke to the owner, Harry Ford. Later he watched from across the street at Ferguson's Restaurant as Booth showed off a horse that he had picked up at a stable. The man he spoke to seemed to be in awe as Booth spurred the horse into a fast gallop down the street just barely missing a fruit vendor who had just entered the street to sell his crop from a push cart. Johnson knew that Booth would be out riding for the next few hours. He would meet a friend and then try to intercept a carriage carrying Ulysses Grant and his wife. Johnson knew this attempt would fail, so he made plans to pick up Booths' trail at the Kirkwood house around 6:00 p.m. In the meantime he ate the last meal he would have in the year 1865.

Booth showed up as stated in the book. Johnson trailed him from Kirkwood's to the alley behind Ford's Theater where he boarded his horse in the theater's stable before walking over to the National Hotel. It was just after 6:45 p.m. and Johnson knew that Booth would not be coming back to the theater until after 10:00 p.m. to commit the act that made him an inseparable part of history, but Johnson needed to be in the box before anyone arrived so he set to the task of gaining admission to it.

He made his way into the theater by telling anyone who asked that he was part of the contingent that would be guarding the President that night. Under this guise he was able to safely reach the Presidential box in the balcony.

For the next few hours he waited as he was doing now. It took all his will to stay concealed when President Lincoln entered the box just after 8:30 p.m. He wanted to jump up and reveal to the President of the plot to assassinate him, but he could not. He had to stop Booth with the gun in his hand for right now Booth could not be convicted of anything; any evidence against him would surely prove to be circumstantial in nature. It could also be easily shown that many bitter men in this time had talked of killing Lincoln, Booth would have just been another one of many.

The band played "Hail To The Chief" when it was known that Lincoln had arrived. This was Johnson's cue to ready himself for the time when Booth would enter the box. By pushing the edge of the partition nearest to the wall out a few inches, Johnson saw that he had the angle he wished. The Presidential party's back was to him. When Booth entered the box, he would be standing directly between them and Johnson.

At 10:15 p.m. Johnson heard the sound of heavy boot steps approaching. Booth entered the box smelling of whisky. Johnson could not help being amazed that none of the party noticed his arrival as they were apparently absorbed in the play. The assassin stood quietly for what seemed to be a long time, but in truth was only a single minute. In that time Johnson emerged from his hiding place behind the partition. As he came up behind Booth he saw that something was terribly wrong. Booth had his pistol out, but it was not aimed at the President, it was aimed at the woman who sat to Lincoln's right.

"Mary." Booth said softly.

As Mary Todd Lincoln turned to face him, Johnson saw the look of fear that came over her. She, and now Johnson, then knew that Booth had come not to kill the President, but to kill her. She was Johnson's mysterious Mary, she was "Mrs. Slater", and she was the secret lover of John Wilkes Booth!

Johnson lunged forward as Booth pulled the trigger. His shoulder hit Booth in the small of the back forcefully knocking the breath out of him as both men hit the floor.

The two of them lay stunned for a few seconds as screams broke out all over the playhouse. Johnson looked up in time to see Mrs. Lincoln take hold of her husband. He could also see the blood flowing from the back of the mortally wounded President's head.

Booth stood up, gasping for breath. He looked at the scene in the box, then to the gun in his hand. Realizing what he did, he dropped the gun and tried to escape while shouting, "I must have my freedom". An Army officer in the box lunged at Booth trying to apprehend him, in the struggle that followed, the officer was wounded. This gave Booth time to get to the railing of the box. He took one last look back at Mary Todd Lincoln who sat sobbing over her dying husband. With a look of unimaginable anguish he jumped from the balcony and into the void of history.

Johnson also ran from the box, now fully aware of his wretched place in history. Startled theater patrons and workers who encountered him saw a madman run by shouting that Lincoln had been shot.

And Johnson kept running. He neither new nor cared where he went; he just wanted to escape from the nightmare he had made for himself. Somehow, in his woe, he managed to find his way back to the Surratt boarding house. As he sat in his attic room he wished only to die as the President was soon to die.

Why had he been such a fool? Why had he tried to change history? Locke was right, time is a wall, insurmountable and unalterable. What has happened is what will always be. You can move the blocks around as he had done, but the wall will look the same. With these thoughts pouring through his mind, Johnson packed his supplies and called the Timatron to him.

He threw himself into it, set the controls to return to his own time, and in a flash he was gone.

On the journey back he thought that the vortex seemed different. Gold became pink, pink became purple, purple became red, then red became gold. The process repeated itself during the entire trip back, a trip that seemed to take longer than usual, but he did not care about any of this. He cared only about escaping.

*   *   *

The laboratory was dark when the journey finally ended, and Johnson was glad of this; he did not feel like being back in the light for a long time. It also meant that his dear friend Locke was not in, which was also fine, he was not sure that he could ever face the man again. He stumbled around in the dark looking for his friend's Easachair. Doing so, he manipulated the chair to full recline, fell into it, and was soon swept off into an erratic sleep.

The next sensation he felt, was someone shaking him, he heard Locke speaking, "Time to wake up you big failure."

Johnson could not open his eyes to face his partner who must have found out that the mission was a shambles.

"Please don't berate me Locke", Johnson pleaded, "I feel terrible enough as it is and you have no idea the depth of my failure."

"Sure I do. When I saw you snoring away in here, I went to look at the history books; nothing has changed! Booth killed Lincoln, the Army killed Booth, and Mary Lincoln became the first female President. It was her actions that changed the course of history. You didn't do anything to alter this."

"What do you mean she became President?" asked Johnson, still not able to look his partner in the eye.

"Just what I said. She was so outraged because of the murder of her husband, she took up his banner and she was elected President. During her time in office she worked feverishly to end prejudice. She banned all state laws against miscegenation and declared that all races should mix with each other. It's generally considered that she is the one who made things better for our kind not Abe Lincoln. Which is why I still don't see how your idea of saving him could have helped us. Why if it weren't for him getting killed she would have not been elected and if it weren't for her, we would have never been allowed to study and become scientists. We would probably be working in a convenience store selling coffee and cigarettes."

"What are you going on about Locke?", asked Johnson, opening his eyes and turning to look at his friend, "That is not how history . . . .".

"History what? You were back there in history, you saw what conditions were like before old Abe was killed; times were terrible for us. Sure its' true that good old Mary Todd was a little crazy. I mean I don't know how anyone could believe all her talk about how a Union soldier helped kill her husband. Still it was just that kind of talk that made enough people stop believing in either side of the Civil War conflict. That allowed her to start her own political party, secure women the right to vote, and then get elected. We were just lucky that she did not go completely off her rocker until after she was out of office. Can you imagine how useless she would have been to us as President if she had been in the Oval Office when she started babbling about how she actually loved John Wilkes Booth and that no one else was suppose to have known about it? No wonder her son put her in an insane asylum."

"No, no, no. This is all wrong, your all wrong. This must be a nightmare."

"A nightmare? What did you get a hold of back in 1865? Some type of hallucinogen? And what the hell are you staring at Johnson?"

"Your face Locke, your face!"

"What's wrong with my face Johnson? Did you forget what I looked liked over time? Ha, ha! Get it pal? 'Over time'! I made that up. Not bad for a man who has no imagination, huh?"

"But you're black! You're black!"

"Come, come, my dear sir, not black. Mulatto! Mulatto in the same combination you are. Daddy was black, mamma was white. Or did you forget all this while you were back in 1865? Heck, your even a little more so than I am with having that mulatto great-granddaddy in your family tree."

"What!? My family tree? What do you mean?"

"Look partner, I am going out to get some breakfast. I want you sobered up by the time I get back. We still have a lot of work to do on that inter-dimensional door before we can sell it to anyone. I mean that last monster we let in was disgusting. I only just did Vapor Ray it in time to stop it from killing us. We need to set up a view port so we can see where we are going first before we go there. Boy, this inter-dimensional travel is not like time travel because we know how time is, don't we? We can come and go in it as we please, right partner?."

As Johnson rose and walked over to the mirror in the lab's restroom he knew how time was. He and the large, muscular, light black skinned stranger who looked back at him knew exactly how time was. It was not a wall, it was fragile mirror and it was not something to throw stones at.

THE END

WOMAN IN BLACK

Debra brushed her hair furiously, threatening to take it out at its roots. Though she knew she had successfully cleaned out all of the sludge that had been in it, she still brushed in case there was even a trace of that giant Tarantula Nebula bacillus entrails left in her shoulder length ash blonde hair. Why did those things stink so badly when they exploded?

Finally satisfied that she could do no more, Debra stepped back to give herself the once over as she did every time she stood in front of a full-length mirror.

Pulling up the strap on her black silk bra, she was happy that her breasts were still firm and round after 35 years of hard living. Her waist was the same size it was in high school—maybe college—while her hips were still sexy and trim enough to attract the stares of men from all ages and planets.

Turning sideways, she did think her rear end was a tad on the large size, but then her black lace silk panties, which she always wore, tended to make it look that way. Fully clothed no one would notice and those who actually saw her scantily clad as she was now never seemed to care. She passed inspection.

Before she began to try on her assignment outfits, she wriggled into a black, knee length silk slip. Her Director had told her it would be cold where she was going and suggested a different undergarment arrangement, but she just could not wear anything else. Unlike him, and all the other men in her profession, she had to constantly change into different styles and colors of outer garments. She could not accommodate wearing just their basic black outfits, so she wore her black "badge" under everything else. She was proud to be a member of the Women In Black.

Not just any WIB though, she thought smugly, as she looked over the contents of the assignment package that had been delivered the day before. She was a WIB Weapons Master, the highest rank available to her, a Certified Eradicator, and a WIB squad leader; she usually pulled the toughest assignments, including the most precarious ones involving time and spatial travel. Those were the types she enjoyed the most since the Society's scientists could transport her not only through time, but through space as well.

Decades earlier, the Society In Black discovered that Earth had been visited many times in the past by creatures from different worlds. While most of these visits were not harmful to the human race, there were some that were real nuisances and had to be dealt with, as long as doing so would not change the present in any way.

Her last assignment had been fairly routine since it took her no farther away than to present day Iquique, Chile where the unauthorized landing of those giant Tarantula Nebula bacilli threatened to scare off the region's robust tourist trade. After eradicating the threat, it was let out that a new form of giant cockroach had emerged from the rain forest; since reports of new life forms from this region were not unusual. So, after the initial terror subsided, the tourist trade went back to normal. It may have even increased as the curious came down to catch a glimpse of these new fiends. Thanks to Debra and her squad, none would ever be seen again.

When she returned home, she was looking forward to the two weeks off that was mandatory for all SIB fighters after an assignment. That is why it was such a surprise when, two days after her arrival home, the Director called her with this new mission. Though he tried to hide it, he could not cover up the agitation in his voice. Debra was sure this was because he was being pressured by someone higher up to put her back into action right away. She knew the Director had feelings for her and she enjoyed his company as well, which is why he was so familiar with her undergarment choices, but they did not let their personal relationship interfere with their work. Still, she felt as though he watched out for her. That meant that whatever business he was being forced to send her on now must be a real "monster" of a project. She giggled at her own joke.

Opening new assignment packages always gave her a thrill. She remembered that it was like opening Christmas presents when she was child. The anticipation was the best part, even if you were given something you really did not want.

The contents of this one consisted of her Assignment Instructions envelope, a few dresses, circa unknown to her, a rather odd dictionary, and the most powerful small arms issued to her group: an Extirpator, complete with leg strap. Yes, this must be a real monster of a project she thought as she hefted the weapon.

As she sat down in her comfortable, overstuffed, lounge chair chills went up and down her spine.

She pulled out her AI and read:

Departure Date/Time:	July 24, 2084—9:27 AM
Return Date/Time:	July 24, 2084—9:28 AM
Destination Entry Code:	Whitechapel /1888/8/27
Length of Assignment:	Maximum stay if necessary

Target:	Jack the Ripper—Origin/Species: Unknown
Weaponry:	Extirpator
Provisions:	Data Pak, Appropriate currency, Dictionary, 1888 attire (High & low Status)
Goal:	ELIMINATION

Mission Impetus:

The SIB Time-Research Team (SIBTRT) has detected a consistent time/occurrence-pattern associated with the appearance of this creature and certain events of a horrific nature that have taken place prior to and since the target time period, leading the SIBTRT team to believe that said "Ripper" is of alien origin.

Since the creature's appearances have been intermittent through time, the SIBTRT is not aware of its present whereabouts or when it will emerge again. The SIBTRT also can only speculate as to where it has been in the past though, when it appears, it follows the same time/occurrence-pattern. The SIBTRT believes that this creature may be the catalyst leading to periods of great fear and death for much of man's history.

The SIBTRT is certain to a 96 percentile that the crimes committed on or near the target date were the workings of this creature due to the fact that another period of unrest occurred just 3 years before this time in a less industrialized area of Earth. Unfortunately, records of those events were not as well documented as they were during the targeted time period. Still, the fact that the undertakings were similar and close together in time, on relatively the same time/occurrence-pattern raises the probability of them being achieved by the same creature.

The goals of this creature are unknown at this time, but due to their appalling nature, SIBTRT feels that the creature's actions may someday lead to the obliteration of Earth itself either as the sole destructor or as the channel which man himself uses to destroy the planet.

Your mission is to eliminate this creature at all costs.

Debra put down the AI sheet, letting the paper rest gently in her lap. "At all costs" meaning even if she were to die trying. While service in the SIB surely had its risks on all assignments, death being one of them, rarely was it spelled out so clearly in an AI!

The team also had to be extremely certain that eliminating this creature would benefit mankind since her assignment called for "Maximum Stay if needed".

Early in SIB's time travel experiments, it found that sending people into another stream of time for a length of time greater than 5 days was fatal. After five days, the agents began to fuse with the time flow they were in. Several unfortunate, and messy, accidents occurred when the SIBTRT team brought someone back who was half fused with the past and half fused with the present. Debra grimaced at the thought of the pictures she was made to view during her training. Now everyone sent back had an automatic retrieval node implanted in the nape of his or her neck. You could not stay more than five days if you wanted to and only rarely did assignments run for more than three days. However, if you ever needed to return earlier, you just had to rub your neck in just the right way to activate the node.

So, she had five days, which should be plenty of time considering the movements and habits of the creature, in the targeted time frame, were fairly well recorded—if she remembered her history correctly. She figured that she should be able to lure the creature in rather easily.

With the departure time in the morning, Debra knew she had to do some fast studying. She pored over her memory for what she knew about Jack the Ripper while reading the accompanying data sent by the SIBTRT.

"Jack" was the infamous murderer of prostitutes in the Whitechapel district of Old London's East End. Though he was credited with killing relatively few people, all his victims were women whom he slashed to death in a bloody, horrific manner which kept the city in the grip of terror for years since he had never been caught. The women he preyed upon were prostitutes; most were forced into their "profession" by poverty. They were part of the criminal underground of that era.

This would explain the dictionary.

Picking it up, she reread the title, "Hanson's Cockney-to-English Dictionary". The Director must have had to dig deep for this one, she thought with a grin. Cockney, said her SIBTRT literature, was the language used by minor criminals of the time. It was a "code" used by them so they could communicate with each other without the law being any wiser. Many of the words and phrases made their way into the popular language of the time.

As she settled down to her studies, Debra was glad that at least one part of this mission would be amusing.

*   *   *

"Very nice, neck down, ya know. The boat race is a problem, but then I don't 'ave to look a' it I 'spose."

Whirling at the comment, the tawdry looking woman retorted, "'oo you talkin' 'bout, guvna? Take a butchers at this. These'll knock yer mincers out."

She then pulled down her neckline showing a wealth of cleavage.

"Ain't neve' said y' ain't got a bit of a body on ya; nice arse an' all. But a plain one y'are, I say. Maybe a bit o' color would dice you up."

"Ain't neve' touched the stuff, an' I ain't gonna start fer the likes of you."

"Oh I'd duck, ya right enough, you witch. But I got ta get home to the trouble 'n strife. Maybe it'll be I'd pass this way again."

"Right, you get to yer troubles, she's got yer by the barnacle bills, she 'as. Go on, get it on 'ome, I got my bees knees to attend to."

The man gave her an angry glance, she tensed, ready to act, but he only cursed at her, pulled the knot tighter around his leather apron, and faded into the fog. Probably heading home for a warm meal and a dry bed; something Debra wished she could do at that moment.

She had been out in the Whitechapel district for two nights now, searching for Jack the Ripper, and so far all she had gotten were lookers and a few "customers" she could not avoid—or so they thought after they woke up. It was impossible to play the part of a prostitute convincingly with out going off with some of the men who approached her and she did not want to attract attention. So, if she were unable to avoid the men who came on to her, she would put her hand to their faces when they were alone letting her Meditation Ring inject a small dose of Atropa Belladonna into them. When they awoke, if they remembered anything at all, it would be a mild hallucination that she was sure their male egos would turn into memories of a good time. She gave any money she "earned" to the real prostitutes who roamed the dark, dank, filthy streets of the East End. Maybe if they had a few more farthings they could go home early and live another day.

Her trip back to 1888 had been flawless as usual. The SIB Time Techs were the best in the business.

They had set her down in dense fog and fading daylight outside a ratty, boardinghouse in the Whitechapel district. Immediately after securing a room, she changed into her "low status" outfit and began to make her rounds, in areas frequented by prostitutes, looking to entice Jack the Ripper into selecting her for his first victim instead of poor Polly Nichols—the Ripper's first known victim. Though many other deaths had been attributed to this creature, the SIBTRT focused on its first verified casualty since Polly's whereabouts were fairly well documented considering the underdeveloped time she had lived in.

It was known that the killer only struck after dark, so during the day, Debra studied her funny dictionary and practiced her unarmed combat techniques. Given the wretched state of her room, she even practiced throwing her razor sharp but quite un-regulation stiletto into one of the house beams. She was getting better at this lost art with each toss. Maybe when she returned to 2084, she could show the Director how effective her technique had become.

He might finally relent and allow all her SIB brothers and sisters carry one. If her mission was successful, she would have that much better of an argument in their favor.

Going back to her room on the dawn of the second day, Debra was disappointed at her inability to quickly find the creature she was sent to eradicate. Normally, she could sense an alien presence in her sleep—a skill that had saved her on more than one occasion. She was having no such luck on this time. It was now, Wednesday, August 29th, 1888 and sometime in the next 24 to 36 hours Jack the Ripper would kill Polly Nichols unless she could stop him. Though this was not her main focus, she wanted to prevent the poor girl from dying the grisly death that was at hand for her.

The plan, as the Director explained to her before she left, was to sniff out this creature and destroy it before it begins its rampage. The impact of this on the immediate history after 1888 had been judged as negligible since none of the women murdered were ever likely to amount to anything nor would their potential offspring, given the kind of life they would be born into. Eliminating any of the destruction and death he was suspected to have caused since his Ripper days, also would not have a severe impact on time and it would lead to a more serene planet.

When Debra returned to her room, she pulled out her data again. After studying it some more, she decided her tactics needed to change. If she were to succeed she would have to look for the creature in a different ways.

She presumed, based on the intermittent appearances of the beast that it was landing then taking off for varying periods of time before returning. It sounded like some sort of territorial hunter that just happened across her solar system. She had run across a few aliens like that in her time with the SIB team, only this one seemed to grow stronger and more expansive through time.

It may have been using a nearby planet as a base to go on foraging excursions to other planets. That meant that it was possible that the monster had not yet landed in 1888.

In that case, this morning, she was going out to watch for it. Now, if she were a hunter preying on an unsuspecting populace, where would she land? Since there were no reports of "men from the moon" around the time she was in, she concluded that it did not want to be seen. With a plan in mind, Debra readied her supplies for the day.

*   *   *

After a while a "better dressed" woman emerged from Debra's room with plenty of silver jangling about in her purse. Her appearance startled the gnarled old housekeeper who had checked her in two days earlier. He looked at her with suspicion, as if he thought that she might have slit a customer's throat for his money. She just flashed him an easy smile, handed him five shillings and asked him to hold her room for a few more days. The sight of the money delivered a grin of jagged, rotting teeth to his face. Before she gagged at the sight, Debra turned and was out the door. Thankful for the clean air of the time, she had to walk a ways to find a cab.

She was fascinated at the different styles of each carriage the cabbies used. Many were very ornate and looked as if they were made with great patience. She finally saw one that looked if it would fit her needs perfectly. It was two-wheel carriage, with two doors that swung outward to allow passengers to get in. The driver actually sat above and behind the passenger area. With the front wide open, Debra would have a wide area of vision.

A magnificent brown horse with a pitch black mane pulled the carriage. Debra thought, teasingly, about swearing the horse in as a temporary SIB member. He was a beautiful creature.

Handing the driver a handful of coins, she hired the cab for the day giving the cabby instructions to go out to the countryside, any countryside, and circle around London as much as he could.

Protesting that he would miss his meal and his tea time, Debra slipped him more money telling him to stop whenever he needed, as she may want to eat too. He still looked reluctant while eyeing the pile of coins in his hand. Finally Debra offered to pay for all his expenses, including meals, for the day. Sensing that he could not do better, the driver relented. With the deal done, she got in the cab and they were off.

As they cleared the city, Debra was amazed at how beautiful the countryside was in comparison to the town. Everything was green and leafy. Small streams ran virtually every which way. She wanted to stop the driver so she could splash in the cold water, maybe even sit soaking her feet in it. She remembered, vaguely, doing just these activities when she was a very young child. Where the stream was located she could not remember, nor could she remember how she had come to the place. Memories from that time in her life often came to her like wisps of dreams and were just as unsubstantial against the background of her current adventurous life. Lately, it seemed to her as if she had always been a SIB member.

Tempting as this childish urge was, she knew she would not give in to it while on a mission or under any circumstances for that matter she thought with a slightly disconsolate feeling. Now she spent most of her time jumping from town to town and time to time in pursuit of threats to mankind. Even during her mandatory two-week breaks she would spend her days at the SIB

Institute of Learning, studying the latest identified life forms while discovering who was friendly and who was an enemy. If they were an enemy, she calculated their weaknesses and weapons. It was because of her dedication to this pastime, that she was fairly certain no being had ever visited Earth which she did not know of—so whatever this Ripper creature turned out to be, she would deal with it.

After a few hours of riding in the cab as she looked for signs of a landing and watched the sky for telltale signs of an incoming ship, the driver pulled up outside of a roadside inn, demanding that she buy him the meal she promised.

With time winding quickly down towards the untimely and gruesome death of Polly Nichols, Debra was reluctant to stop, but she did make the man a promise. She decided to walk a ways from the inn as he ate, since she had no appetite.

Approaching the edge of a nearby forest, she did not to enter it. The trees were so tall and beautiful that she actually felt intimidated by their presence; a feeling that no man, woman, or alien had been able to make her feel in many years. Skirting the edge of the forest, she kept the cab within her eyesight lest the driver run off and leave her stranded miles from town.

She made a vow to herself to go somewhere and visit a forest in her own time on her next leave. There had to be one somewhere. Maybe they were not as large and pristine as this forest, but at least it would be one that she could walk in.

When the driver emerged from the inn, she decided to change tactics once again. It seemed futile to keep searching for her target in this slow means of transportation, so she asked the driver to take her back to her rooming house. If she could not find the creature, she decided to let the creature find her. But this time, she would use better bait.

*   *   *

"An' oo' are you, to be askin' for Miss Polly?"

"Like I tolds ya, I'm a friend o' 'ers, I am"

"Y'ain't no friend, I knows Miss Polly, she y'ain't got no friend like yerself."

"I's from outa town, I is. I know'd her when we was a couple o' whelps, I did."

"Well, she never'd mentioned yer likes before, but ya look 'armless enough, ya do. Miss Polly said she was goin' over to the Fryin' Pan since wasn't 'avin too many goes out 'ere. That'd be over on Brick, since yer not from 'ere."

Debra thanked the lady and passed her a few pence for her information. This gesture earned Debra another rotten toothed grin.

It was now 1:12 AM. She had been staying as close to Polly as she could, using information the SIBTRT had gleaned from records made by the police regarding the woman's whereabouts on this dreadful night. Debra found that the information was lacking or just plain wrong in some areas, but still, she was able to have a pretty good idea where Polly was most of the time. She had spotted her three times only to lose her in the howling rain that was coming down. Thunder and lighting, like she had never seen before, made conversation with others on the street almost impossible. She dared not go ahead of Polly, to wait for her, since there may have been an unrecorded detour on her path to death. So Debra followed as best she could while fighting the weather and fending off men who wanted to be with her for the night.

As she reached the Frying Pan, she saw Polly leaving. She followed her to a rooming house on Thrawl and waited until she saw Polly being thrown out of the building while cursing and yelling at a man who appeared to be the proprietor. For the next hour, she pursued Polly as she staggered along in the rain trying desperately to catch the eye of potential customers. She stopped once to talk to a lady who seemed disgusted at Polly's desolate state but did not care to help her change it in anyway.

Soon it would be time for Debra to put her plan into action.

At 3:00 AM, Debra caught up to Polly as she staggered to a stop, leaning heavily against the wall of a building on Buck's Row.

"Polly." she said, dropping her Cockney accent.

"'oo's there?" Polly said, looking about in the dark, "'oo's callin' f' Polly?"

Stepping forward where she could be seen, Debra replied, "My name is Debra, I want to help you."

"'elp me you say?" Polly asked as she eyed Debra warily, "'oo are you? Why da ya want ta 'elp me? I don' need, yer 'elp anyway."

"Do you need your doss money for the night, Polly?"

"Why yer askin' that for? An' what kind o' lingo yer speakin' there?"

"I am speaking English, Polly. Just a different form of it than you are used to hearing. I want to help you get out of this awful weather. I want you to go somewhere safe and dry for the night. There is danger on the streets of London tonight and I don't want you to be caught up in it."

"Why'd ya care about me, I don'ts even know ya? Yer not one o' them preachers are ya?"

"No Polly, I am not a preacher. I am just someone who is interested in making sure you are safe. Don't ask me why, Polly. You must believe me that I only have your interests in mind. Why else would I approach you like this."

Polly sagged back against the wall. "I don't know, I don't know. Why'd anybody have ol' Polly in mind." She began to weep, piteously.

Debra put a hand to her shoulder in comfort while noting the time on her watch. It was 3:05 AM; if she had to, she would knock Polly out and leave her someplace warm and dry. But no matter what she had to do, the only woman who was going to meet Jack the Ripper this night was Debra. It would not be this pathetic woman standing in front of her.

"Look, Polly. Here is a pound for you."

"A pound, ya say?" Polly asked, suddenly looking sober.

"Yes. Take it, take it and go back to that place on Thrawl Street and stay for a week. That would show that mean old owner."

Polly's eyes darted one way up the street, then down the other. She snatched the money from Debra's hand. Stashing the money somewhere in a pocket, she stood up straight and tried to make something out of the mess of her wet clothes.

"Mebbe I wills and mebbe I's won't. I'va mind to take my bees knees elsewhere, I does."

With that, Polly turned away and headed to relative safety. That left Debra alone to face the creature that awaited its victim.

*   *   *

A cold alien feeling engulfed her. So the SIBTRT was right, Jack the Ripper was not human. No human ever had a presence like this.

Ducking down to one knee, she looked about her. It was dark, but the rain had stopped, so the night was clear. Her senses were aflame, like that of a hunter after its prey. She listened for a footfall on the cobblestone, but none came. She looked about for movements in the shadows, but there was none to be seen. Reaching under her dress, she pulled out her Extirpator. The weapon felt small and weightless in her hand, but she knew that it could knock a flying ship from the sky with one shot. Her heart pounded as the alien feeling thickened in the air around her. She felt herself actually getting goose—bumps! Where was this being? Her answer came from above.

A face, that of a demon, appeared in the air, perhaps twenty feet off the ground. It's complexion was red, its ears tapered upward to a sharp point, two horns grew just above its forehead, and the tiny goatee that grew to a point on its chin was the only hair on its head. She had seen this face before, but where she could not remember.

"Human", the face said, the word hung, spelled out, in the air like smoke after a fire.

Debra did not answer.

"Human", it said again, louder. Again Debra remained mute. She was not one to be scared by parlor tricks, especially when she was facing the enemy.

She thought about poor Polly. If she had come across this monstrosity, she would be terrified beyond speech. She may have even died of fright where she stood.

Getting no reaction obviously perturbed the monster. The face grew redder and became more substantial, rounding out like that of a real person.

"Human!", it said, this time the word shook the ground under Debra.

Fire came out of its nostrils, smoke flowed from its ears, and its eyes lit up like those of a jack-o-lantern. What a sight. Debra could not help herself, she laughed out loud!

This really set the creature off. A body, some 20 feet tall, began to form under the head. It was as red as the face, had cloven hooves for feet, and had a cute, thought Debra, pointy little tail. She laughed again.

The creature began to stomp its hooves, shaking nearby buildings. Debra, afraid that they would fall and hurt someone, decided to end her little game and get rid of this clown at the same time. Gripping her Extirpator while hiding it in the folds of her clothes, she stood up, ready to act.

"Okay, Jack. Enough with the feet stomping. You might actually hurt someone."

The monster immediately ended his distressful little dance. He seemed puzzled, almost angry, at the fact Debra was not afraid of him.

"You will die tonight for your sins, Human!", it bellowed.

"Which sin will you choose, Jack? Should I give you a list of them or do you want to guess?" Debra giggled.

"You make merry, Human?"

"Sure, Jack. I'm just a lonely little girl who is new in town. I have to entertain myself somehow."

"You shall die a painful death for that, Human!", a giant pitch fork appeared in his hands. He raised it menacingly toward Debra.

"Look Jack, before you skewer me, can you tell me one thing? What planet are you from? I know most of you oddballs by sight, but your little magic show here is something I have never seen before. You must be from several galaxies away."

Her words seemed to shrink the alien. There definitely was less intimidation in his appearance. It was as if she had thrown a bucket of water on the creature. He began to slowly rise upwards, so now all its body was floating in the night air.

"You know not who I am, Human?", his voice was less loud.

"No I don't know specifically who you are, but I would guess you were some sort of pod from beyond Polarissima Australis. How long have you been on Earth anyway?"

"But I am the Devil.", it almost whimpered, "I am Lucifer, Beelzebub, Satan." The last word was a shout. With each name it spoke, the creature seemed to regain its sense of importance.

Debra remembered now. This was a mythical creature that millions of humans still believed in back in her own time. She recalled that her own parents had believed in this being and his nemesis, God. But if there was such a thing as the Devil, this was not he. This was a charlatan in evil-ones clothing and he was not fooling someone like Debra who had seen more than her share of peculiar creatures.

"Save it for the locals, Jack. I don't believe in you. I know you come from another planet, so why don't you name where in case I run across a buffoon like you again?"

"How do you know these things, Human? How do you know of creatures from beyond your world? You are not to know these things!", it shouted, panic rising in its voice.

"You tell me first, Jack! Maybe we can share some secrets."

"No! You say unto me how thou knows these things!"

"What's with the lingo, Jack. Get tired of speaking English?"

"You shall die tonight!", it raised its pitch fork again, ready to slay Debra. But she shot first. Right into the creatures gaping mouth. To her amazement, the creature was not vaporized; the shot had passed right though it.

Still, it did put down its weapon and shrink to her height. It seemed curious about the Extirpator. As it strode forward, now no sound came from it hooves as they struck the pavement. Debra dared not shoot again. If the ray went through it again, she would destroy blocks of buildings behind it.

Reaching under her dress, she pulled out her stiletto and attacked the creature before it could take another step. She could not believe it when she found herself on the other side of it. She had gone through it was if it were nothing more than a beam of light!

Turning back to the creature, she found it floating over her once more.

"You will come with me.", it roared.

Before she could respond, she found herself being lifted off the ground, chest first, by an unseen force. She held on to her weapons as if they might save her should she be released.

She could see the beast in front of her as they rose, but she could see no destination. Where was this thing taking her? The first real feelings of fear began to creep up on her.

From nowhere, a black, yet almost transparent, cloud came up and dulled the light from the stars behind it. It must have been some kind of ship, but not one that she had ever seen or heard about in her studies.

She would have to catalog it if she survived. With that academic thought twisting in her mind, she was pulled inside.

* * *

She floated in the darkness for what seemed to be a long time. But checking her lighted watch she realized it had not been more than a few minutes. The pitch blackness inside the craft gave her no sense of motion, thus no sense of time. Checking her watch also made her realize that her time in 1888 was running out. Soon the autoretreival system in her neck would take her back to 2084.

She did find that she could move her limbs while being pulled along, so she stashed her weapons back under her dress and mentally readied herself for whatever this creature had planned for her.

She soon found out what this would be. The force that pulled her along released its grip, and though she did not think it was really happening, she felt herself falling. It was the kind of feeling you had in a dream. You were afraid, but somewhere you knew that you would soon wake up. Debra desperately wanted to wake up. Ahead of her, a bright light appeared. She was rushing towards it at a great speed now. When she knew she was about to enter the light source, she closed her eyes tightly. Opening them, she found herself laying flat on her back in a pit of fire! The feeling of falling had left her completely.

The creature floated onto a rough hewn throne made of some kind of stone. Sitting itself down, he raised his hands bringing the flames up higher and, though they were hot, they did not burn her. It was as if someone suddenly turned up the heat in a sauna. Then a stench entered the chamber that made her gag. It has the smell of rotten, real rotten, eggs. She steeled her senses to the odor. The creature lifted one hand raising her as he did. He spun his hand around slowly causing Debra to cartwheel in the air. Again, she began to feel a shiver of fear creeping up her spine. As if the creature sensed this, he spun her faster and increased the size of the flame, the smell became even more putrid.

Debra's mind was working feverishly to keep her dread in check and to keep her equilibrium normal. She kept telling herself that this was only a space creature. She had met and destroyed, when needed, many just like it. This one was a little different though in that it seemed to know humans intimately while for the majority of the aliens she had encountered, this was not so.

"Human", its voice thundered in the chamber, "Tell me how you know of creatures from beyond your world."

"I-just-know", she choked out in response. She was starting to lose the battle. What was this monster? Could he really be Satan? Could there be such a being?

Her spinning stopped with a jolt. The creature lifted her higher, transporting her above the flames in the chamber. It stopped her over metal table. Flipping

her, it began to lower her on to device. She braced herself for the searing pain
the hot metal would cause, only to be surprised when the table was cold to the
touch. Her outer garments flew off of her leaving her lying on the apparatus in
only her underwear. Her slip hid her weapons.

Unseen straps clamped around her wrists, ankles, and waist. She felt invisible
"hands" begin to probe her up one side and down the other, both front and
back. When the hands reached certain areas, she had to stifle the urge to giggle
or moan. During the ordeal, her mind raced, scanning what she could see,
looking for an escape route of some kind. All the while, the things being done
to her, reminded her of the UFO history taught to her in SIB training. There
were many reports of abduction and probing just like this, with varying special
effects reported, that had never been explained. Maybe it was because people
were looking at the sky above and not in the Earth below them?

Abruptly the hands stopped their exploration. The creature flew from his
seat and floated just inches above her prostrate body. Up close, the sight of it
was truly terrifying. She noticed the pock marked skin of its face and the scars
on its body that looked like they were caused by constant contact with stone.
She began to wonder if she was wrong? Was this really Hell? It fit all accounts
of it that she had heard. But if someone were to be put here, they surely could
not escape, so how did anyone really know what Hell was like?

"Human", it rasped.

As it spoke, its mouth opened revealing that its tongue had became a
serpent. Holding its mouth open, the beast grazed her faced then moved
lasciviously down her body. It wrapped itself around her breasts, squeezing
them as if it were choosing melons in a grocery store. Floating downward, she
felt the beast tickling her navel, then she felt it at the hem of her slip. It lifted it
upward and began to trace the line of her underwear.

Debra wanted to vomit, but could not. Her breath came in short gasps,
she wanted to tremble but her body was held tight by the invisible clutches of
the creature. This is it, this really is Hell. Jack the Ripper was really the Devil.
That is why he was never caught. That is why he came and went with no
pattern except one of unspeakable evil. Debra wanted to die, anything to get
out.

"Human", it roared as it shot upwards from her. It grew to its enormous
size again.

"Human speak now or die!"

Debra tried to respond, but could not get any words out.

"Then thou shalt die in Hades, o sinful one."

As it raised its hand, the pitch fork materialized once more, Debra could
not think of anything to do. She was helpless and she knew it. Death was just
moments away. Her thoughts went back to the times in her childhood, when

her mother used to speak of this being. She had feared it even though she had never seen it. Debra knew now, first hand, why she did. Her mother would shake and moan with dismay at the thought of the Devil while finding solace only when she spoke of the graciousness of God, that almighty being who, according to her mother, always prevailed over the Devil. She remembered the words, her mother spoke.

"God help me", Debra managed to whisper as the giant pitch fork flew towards her fragile body.

*   *   *

"You rang?", said a little man who popped up out of nowhere. With his appearance, the pitch fork, the Satanic being, and the flames engulfing her all vanished. It was as if she had awoken from a horrible nightmare.

She found herself lying on a cold metal deck of what appeared to be a ship of some sort. She was free to sit up and she was fully clothed again.

Standing before her was, at best, a milquetoast looking little man in a t-shirt that looked as if it belonged to a very bad launderer. It had bright splotches of dye all over it. The markings were uniform only in that they all had a dark spot in the middle of them surrounded by a sunburst of the same color. They were a riot of different sizes.

His pants were bizarre as well in that they had the oddest looking swell to them. The legs actually became wider as they approached the floor so she could just make out the leather sandals on his sock less feet. He was also in need of a hair cut. The word "hippie" came to her mind from somewhere deep in her memory. What did she remember about them?

At best he looked like something out of a museum. His receding hairline and his round, rimless, darkened, spectacles added to his comical look.

"Who are you?" she stammered.

"I am the being whom you called upon."

"You're . . . God?"

"I am a being that has been given that name by the people of your race. Though I am called many things; some call me Allah, others call me Buddha. It makes no difference, I am all of them."

Debra's head was reeling. She had just been accosted by the Devil, now "God" stood before her.

"But you don't look—."

"I don't look like God? I know, I know. I hear that all the time. So tell me, what does God look like?"

Debra's mind pored over all the depictions she had seen of that being. They were all very stately, evoking enormous strength.

"Maybe you think I should look like this?", he said as his image appeared to morph into a tall man with a muscular build, flowing white hair and deep blue, gentle eyes. He was robed in only a white cloth that draped from one shoulder to just above his knees. The image floated just above the floor.

"Or perhaps I should look like this?" he then changed into a short, squat, figure with an oriental face. He wore a robe open to his belly button, showing his enormous girth. A funny hat of sorts sat upon his head.

In the next instant he was back to being a funny looking little man.

"Did you think that was groovy, baby? I can do a lot more tricks like that if you like, but I am not as good as my bud Willie is at these things. Then again, he's the 'techie' between the two of us. He's always playing with his computers, their motherboards and his flash ROM drives to enhance his powers. He has a real precocity with those things. But I guess I don't have to tell you that after the show he put on for you tonight! Me, though, I just don't dig that kind of heavy metal action."

Debra stifled the urge to giggle at this little man when she remembered what happened after she giggled at the other one this one referred to as Willie.

Instead, she played for time. "If you're name is not really God, then what is it?"

"Oh, it is a long, complicated string of characters and numbers, as you would see it, which would make no sense to you. So, in this place, I've chosen the human name of Harold. I like the way it sounds and I think it fits me well, don't you?"

"Yes, quite well. You look very much like someone who should be called Harold. It is a very nice name. My name is Debra. But if you are God then you know that."

"No I didn't know that. Why would I? Debra? What an unusual name. How do you spell that?"

"D-e-b-r-a", she responded, wanting to placate Harold, "I thought God knew everything".

"While I know great many things, I don't follow your rap, lady."

"I'm sorry Harold," she replied meekly.

Looking her over he said, "You are an oddball, for sure. I don't remember a specimen quite like you."

The creature then turned to address a wall at the far end of the room they were in, "Hey Willie, haul it out here, will you."

Suddenly a door appeared and from behind it came an even smaller man who was, in every of respect, Harold's identical twin. He was just as oddly dressed.

"What is it, Harold? I have to do a hard reboot of my system now that you pulled the plug on it. Why'd you do that anyway? You know what a bummer that is for me." This new little man seemed very perturbed.

"Because that's the rules of the game man, if someone calls for me, I win."

"But I didn't hear her, dude." Harold whined.

"Of course not, you were too busy playing with your holograms and tractor beams to pay attention. But I heard her, so I win. So quit being such a downer."

"Yeah, yeah, whatever. No need to get uptight about it, dude. I'll get you next time."

Harold looked like a child who was just given a bit of candy; Debra expected him to jump with sheer joy.

"Anyway, Harold, what do you want now? I have to boogey on back to the lab."

"This one you brought on board is a real strange one. Could these beings have had an evolutionary deviance that we didn't track?"

Willie sat down on the bulkhead, chin in hands, seemingly to ponder the question. After just a few seconds, he popped back up to his feet.

"No Harold, I'm sure that I've got'em all. Maybe she is just a quirk in evolution like those big lizards we made. Remember those freakazoids?"

"I remember!," Harold shouted excitedly as he turned to Debra, "We always take on the image of the beings we conjure up and Willie always likes playing the meanest and oddest looking of the creatures, just like that Devil dude of his.

You should have seen him as a lizard! He was huge, taller than most of the others we made. He had a big mouth with rows and rows of sharp teeth. He could run like the wind, but then he had these tiny little limbs on the upper part of his body."

"Hey, I needed to be able to operate my computers!"

"I know Willie, but what a sight you were! Anyway, it was ginchy while it lasted. Remember how hacked off we were when they didn't evolve like we wanted to? Everything grew on the darn things except their intellect. We finally had to destroy them all with that mind blowing firestorm."

"Yeah, that was outasight and sad at the same time", chimed in Willie.

"Oh well, if nothing else, we put on the biggest barbecue in all the galaxies we've ever created!"

At that, they both laughed hysterically.

Debra stood in quiet wonderment. She didn't know what to make of this odd pair! They were certainly creatures from another world and so scientifically advanced that they could create new life forms, but at the same time they seemed so backward. They spoke of computers which she remembered from her history books as an old form of the Plasma Based Analytical Engines in use now. And no one used the old hologram technology anymore, not since the invention of the Mind Projection Cap. She recognized their speech patterns as being antiquated as well. Many of their words and phrases, not to mention their dress, came out of a time before the turn of the last century, she wanted to say they spoke as people did during the 1960's, but there were also traces of the 1970's and 1980's as well. These two were a pair of walking text books.

As quickly as their hysteria started, it stopped. They stared at each other for a moment as if they were trying to read each other's thoughts.

Turning to look at Debra while speaking simultaneously and stroking their chins in rhythm, they asked aloud, "What kind of creature could this be?"

Again they turned to each other and went through the staring routine.

"Willie tells me you spoke of creatures from other planets and tried to use an advanced type of weapon on him when he picked you up?"

"Yeah!" shouted Willie, "Where the heck did you get that zapper thing anyway? You would've fried me if it really had been me out there!"

"Tell us how you know of these things?" Harold demanded, suddenly more schooled in his language and tone of voice. His eyes turned red and threatening as he asked the question.

Not knowing exactly how to respond, Debra chose the truth.

"Well, in the time that I come from, people in my profession deal with aliens all the time. We have amassed a vast knowledge of other planets, other species, and their lifestyles. In this time, such things are not known. I am from the future. Outside of this ship, or whatever it is, the year is 1888, but I am from the year 2084, almost 200 years from this time. I came back in time to deal with a problem."

"Explain.", they said in unison, "What you speak of is not possible."

"No, it is true. About 25 years ago, in my time that is, around 2059, the group I am a member of invented a time-space machine. It can put anyone back in time at any place they choose. They sent me back in time to investigate a creature dubbed Jack the Ripper."

The two small men turned to each other again.

Harold spoke as they turned back to Debra, "As remarkable as we know our creatures are we cannot believe that they have advanced so greatly in just 200 Terran years. We have tracked our creatures and have made different versions of them as needed to help in their intellectual development, but we would never advance them as far as you say you are. We would destroy them first before they could become too powerful and developed the ability to destroy us."

"So, you really can't see beyond this time?"

Willie spoke this time, "We see only what is before us, as our creatures can. It isn't possible to see as you suggest. Now explain your knowledge of creatures from outside your world. This time tell the truth."

"It is the truth!" she said, "I know about beings from other planets because I have met them in the future."

"You lie!" he cried out.

Debra, remembering who she was and realizing that there was little time for her left in 1888, became indignant at the suggestion by this pipsqueak alien that she would lie to him.

"Look, I don't care what you two think. It is as I said it is. If you don't believe me, that is up to you. I am tired and I have to finish the job I was sent here to do."

In the back of her mind, she wondered if she really could do what was needed to complete her mission. It would be one thing to destroy a couple of inane aliens, but these two creatures really appeared to be the God and the Devil beings that billions of people believed in now and in the future. What would it do to the flow of time if she eliminated them?

"Anyway, if anyone here is lying, it is you two."

Looking as if she had just kicked them, they turned to each other to perform the strange staring ritual again.

Turning back, they spoke as one again, "Explain!"

"Okay, but make a note of this or download it onto your floppy disc, I don't care." Debra smiled at her little history joke, "You must be lying to me about not being able to see the future. I mean, sure, you look like something out of the future in *this* era. But where I come from, you're something out of *my* past. Your words, your phrases, your equipment, are all known facts in the history books of my time. You act like a couple of hippies playing with your old PC's. If you can't see the future, how do you know of all these things?"

They immediately snapped sideways to stare at each other. This time the staring ceremony went on for what seemed like forever, but was most likely only a minute or so.

They simultaneously broke the silence, shouting aloud at each other, not paying attention to Debra.

"Contamination!"

Harold started pacing back and forth quickly, not taking more than four steps before turning around and pacing the other way.

"Stop it, Harold. Stop it. It is your fault that this happened."

"Me? It is you who is always experimenting with these beings. You're always testing them for mental strength, always killing the weak ones and releasing the strong ones. Obviously, in the future, some of these test cases contaminated their time. Now they will become too advanced for us to control due to your foolishness."

Willie's head became large and distorted as he listened to Harold's accusation. Finally, he roared back, his head now twice the size of Harold's, "My foolishness? The experimental creatures I use never see me as I am. These beings only see my Devil character. The ones I choose to release go out and tell stories of Hellfire and brimstone or start massive wars. Just as they have for centuries. Moreover, most of the creatures I use are of the self-deprecating class, like the ones that sell their flesh for pleasure to others, so they have little credibility to begin with. You are the one who goes out among the masses in your human form. You dress like them, you eat their food. You have long talks with them. My scientific findings aren't enough for you. No, you need to find out how they are developing emotionally as well, so you speak to them as you speak to me. In the future you must go out in our tribal garb as well since this one has seen it before. From that she must have deduced that we are of the Hipparthian race."

Harold was about to say something, but Willie cut him off.

"Don't deny it. I know you are bigger, stronger, and more powerful than I am, you being the pilot and me just being the co-pilot, but you can't mask everything from me. I know that you have had secret meetings with these beings, I know you have even engaged in intimate relations with them and bore the females children."

Harold flashed a shocked and embarrassed looked at his friend.

"That's right Harold. I know. You can fool these creatures with that 'immaculate conception' absurdity, but did you really think that would get past me? You must have let words, phrases, and knowledge slip out while you were with these cheap women. They in turn must have told your offspring. These bits and pieces knowledge must all come together sometime in the future. Knowing how you are, you probably fall in love with one of the female creatures and tell her everything anyway. You're the contaminant. You're the problem!"

As they screamed at each other, they ignored Debra. She took the opportunity to step back from them, getting as far away as she could.

Harold, meanwhile, shrank at Willie's words. He was very fretful by the time his co-pilot finished.

"Perhaps you are right, my friend, my partner, but it is of no matter which of us caused the contagion, we must now end this experiment. We will have to start over once more."

The thought of this action seemed to pain Willie. He moaned, "But I have so many gigabytes of data! What am I going to do with it if we destroy these creatures?"

"We can use that data to improve the next lot, Willie. We can start over as we have done for eons."

"But I don't want to start over . . ."

"Yet we have to. Do you want them all to end up as this one? ", he said as he nodded in Debra's direction, "You know what must be done."

They had not yet noticed that she had moved away from them, but as she listened in horror, she understood exactly what these creatures were getting at; they meant to destroy the human race!

"You're right, as usual, Harold. We have to do what we have to do, but can we start an entirely new world this time? Can we blow up this planet then bang some particles together in the lab and make another one? I am tired of dealing with this world."

"A splendid idea my friend, "Harold answered, "Lets do just that, and this time we will take longer than six cycles to complete it, I mean we don't have to take a break. Besides, I think we may have rushed this one."

Debra felt as if she had been struck, hard, in the stomach. They were going to destroy Earth and the human race. They talked as if her world was just a batch of bacteria gone bad in a Petri dish. They were going to flush the world down a drain and start all over again. She pulled out her Extirpator. What should she do? She might be able to stop them, but should she kill "God" and the "Devil"? What would happen to time if she did, she thought again? Would her world be different when she returned? If she could return! To do nothing meant the end of everything, no future, no past, her life and the lives of countless millions would be wiped out. Oh, why was a decision like this left up to poor a simple working girl like her?

As these thoughts raced through her mind, she felt herself getting light-headed which was the first sign that her autoretrieval device had kicked in. In a few minutes she would be back in 2084—if it was still there! She had to act.

Raising her weapon, she whispered, "God help me."

The words caused Harold to turn sharply towards her! As he was about to speak, she fired. In an instant, Harold turned to dust. Willie shrieked at the sight of his disintegrated companion. He turned to her with murder in his eyes.

Debra felt herself becoming insubstantial, so she fired once more. Willie now joined Harold as a pile of dust on the bulk head, their remnants mingling. They were together again for eternity as friends should be.

As she swirled away into the black void of time, she remembered something she heard somewhere in some time, "Ashes to ashes, dust to dust . . ."

*   *   *

It was a wedding. Everything and everyone was black and white except for Debra. She was not noticed. She went unseen as she approached a pair of guests standing outside of the church. They were talking.

"She had a lot of nerve wearing white—someone in *her* profession."

"Well it is the world's oldest they say, but still I never thought the Director would go for someone like her; then again there were always the rumors . . ."

"Yes, yes, and now we know they're true, he enjoys paying women for his pleasure, he can command them that way."

"I wonder what he is paying her now?"

That brought a snicker to each of the speakers.

"Too bad he didn't settle down with . . . what was her name, the one that disappeared?"

"Debra something-or-the-other, but it's doubtful that he ever loved her. There was always speculation about why he sent her on that last dangerous mission. You've heard the story how on a night, after one of his heavy drinking fits, he said something to his assistant about finally getting out from under her. I suppose we will never know unless he talks openly about it—which is unlikely now."

Just then the Director and his bride emerged from the chapel. People threw rice and bird seed. He looked around and waved smiling happily, shaking hands with the men, until his gaze crossed the spot where Debra stood. He froze as if he had seen a ghost. Could he see her?

His bride tugged at him to go, but he stood as still as the fabled men who had looked upon Medusa, apparently staring vacantly at an empty space. His bride became impatient, she threw back her veil to say something to the Director, and then she too stood transfixed, staring at the same spot as her new husband.

Debra stared, too, for standing next to the Director, her friend and lover, stood a young Polly Nichols—or at least a distant relative of hers.

Her eyes began to fill with tears as the scene before her began to deconstruct. Time was coming apart at the seams. Large black rifts spiraled downward from the sky, shattering the picture of bliss. Just before she felt the Earth open under her, one of the clefts tore the Director away from his bride.

"So much for 'happily ever after'.", she thought as time engulfed her once more.

*   *   *

"Oh my dear sweet God Jupiter", Debra thought as she looked in the mirror, "This skin tight jump suit sure makes my hips look big."

Turning sideways, made her feel better. Her behind was firm and lovely. Black leather always made it look that way.

Looking at her sales packet, she was happy that the Director was her friend and her lover. He knew that she cherished visiting AquaTerra properties and so he always sent her on these sales calls when one needed to be shown. The ocean floor was always so lovely and he knew that one day she hoped to live there. Her fondest prayer was that she would get a glimpse of mighty Neptune, her favorite of the many Gods.

"Oh, well," she thought, "I had better quit daydreaming and get 'swimming', time is much too precious to waste."

She giggled at her own joke.

THE END

ONE SMALL PLAY ABOUT GOD

STAGE DIRECTIONS

Act 1, Scene 1

(House is in total black out, curtains are open, but nothing can be seen. Slowly the lights come up revealing a man, dressed entirely in black, standing in the middle of a bar room that is not quite complete. Only two stools are visible, the mirror on the wall behind it is askew, cases of liquor remain unopened. The man is casually gazing somewhere between stage right and the audience, left hand on hip.)

MAN: (Normal tone of voice, questioning) "Is God dead?"

MAN: (Shouting now, hands in the air, stepping towards and addressing the audience) "I asked 'Is God dead?'"

(Entering quickly, stage left, a beautiful woman wearing a pure white mini-skirt, cut well above the knee and a tight white blouse. He hands are spread apart.)

WOMAN: "Are you crazy?" (Quick aside to the audience, whispering) "He's crazy!"

MAN: "I heard that! I heard what you said! I am not crazy!"

WOMAN: "You are too! Who else but a crazy man would ask such a question?"

MAN: (With a sly look and sarcastic tone of voice) "How do you even know that I am a 'man'? So far, in our universe here, there is only you and I. How do you know that you are not the man and I am the woman?"

WOMAN: (Moving closer to MAN, poking her hand into his chest, speaking sarcastically) "Don't try to change the subject, buster! You're still crazy. You of all people should know that God is not dead."

MAN: (Quizzically) "Really? Why should I know that?"

WOMAN: (Spitefully) "Because, you fool, if God is dead, then who created you?"

MAN: (Angrily) "You half-wit! And you call me crazy? Don't you realize that we were both created just a few minutes ago by some drunken, jerk-water, writer who has nothing better to do than play God?"

WOMAN: (Shaking with rage and religious vilification) "You are not only blasphemous, your ignorant as well!"

MAN: (Casually turning away from WOMAN) "Don't tell me. Tell God—whoever he may be in your tiny little mind." (Makes a throwaway gesture with his right hand.)

WOMAN: (Backing away from the MAN as if in fear, pointing to the floor, voice rising) "I will tell him. I will tell him to damn you to Hell for your indiscretions."

MAN: (Turning back to WOMAN) "And just how do you plan to do that?"

WOMAN: "Do what?"

MAN: "Are you dense? (Looking up at the ceiling, turning his back on the WOMAN and shouting in an exasperated tone of voice) Couldn't you have written this character a little smarter? Did you have to fill my lonely existence with a brainless, sexy bimbo, (glancing back at WOMAN then back up to the ceiling) with nice legs?"

WOMAN: (Walking around to face MAN) "Now who are you talking to?"

MAN: "I am talking to our Creator. That person that made you and I."

WOMAN: "Then you admit there is a Creator." (Turning to look at the audience, addressing them in a snooty tone of voice, one hand on hip.) See I was right."

MAN: (Abruptly, quickly, anxiously, voice rising) "I never said that there wasn't Creator. I never said that! You weren't right about anything!"

WOMAN: "But you did question his existence. You asked if God was dead?"

MAN: "And I still ask it."

WOMAN: (Shaking again with religious fervor, hands on hips, while stomping her foot one time) "Oh, you are the most infuriating man I have ever known."

MAN: "Of course! I am the only man you have ever known, and unless our moronic Creator sees fit to people it up a little in here, I will be the only one you will ever know."

WOMAN: (Turns her back and begins to hum—no specific tune—arms folded tapping her toe.) "I'm not listening to you." (Continues to hum.)

MAN: "Is that your answer? Just shutting your eyes and ears to the truth?"

(WOMAN continues to ignore MAN, this time by starting to dance, gliding around the stage.)

MAN: (Again looking up at the ceiling) "Will you get her out of here, please? Send me someone who can carry on a lucid dialogue for pity's sake. (Throwing up his hands) Better yet, just erase us. Put us out of our miserable existence."

WOMAN: (Stopping her dance mid-stride and turning meekly towards MAN. Speaking in a docile, quivering tone.) "Wh—wh—why would you ever ask for something like that to happen? Is your life so empty that you would wish for it to end?"

MAN: (Spreading hands full apart to shoulder level, while looking around the set, voice rising) "My life? What life do you speak of? This? This standing in a half empty saloon with a beautiful woman arguing the existence of God? This—this is not life!"

WOMAN: "But you must have something outside of this room? Is there no one?"

MAN: "No. No one. I have nothing and neither do you."

WOMAN: (Balking at this revelation and crossing her arms just under her bosom) "Don't get me caught up in your sick little world! I have a life. I have meaning."

MAN: (Crosses his arms and taps his foot) "Oh? Then do pray tell me about your wonderfully enriching life. What hobbies do you have? What is your favorite color? Are you married—with children? How old are you? How do you like your sex? Come now, do fill me in on the facts that make up your little world."

(WOMAN opens her mouth, makes a pointing gesture as if she is about to speak, then pulls back, thinking, one hand over her chest, one crooked finger at the side of her mouth. Looking very puzzled.)

MAN: "Cat got your tongue? (Exasperated, MAN looks up at the ceiling again, not changing his position) Please! Must you make me speak in clichés? Must you?"

WOMAN: "Will you stop talking to the ceiling? And no, a cat does not have my tongue. I just (hesitating) can't think of anything right now. Perhaps I have a spot of amnesia. (Speaking excitedly) Yes, that is it. I have amnesia! Soon I will remember everything and then I will tell you." (Stands straight up in triumph).

MAN: (Groaning and looking up at the ceiling again still not changing his posture) Must you bring all your idiotic made-for-TV plot twists, your empty chestnuts, and your vapid fantasy girls together at one time? Why do you torture me like this?"

WOMAN: (Also looking up at the ceiling.) "Again, who are you talking to? Is that God?"

MAN: "Yes. (Again looking up at the ceiling, speaking angrily.) Will you please let me out of this idiotic stance? I am getting a cramp. (Relaxing and facing WOMAN while flexing his hands, arms, and shoulders) Yes that is God! As far as you and I are concerned, the person I am talking to is God. He knows all, see all, does all. It is just unfortunate that he is also a lazy, worthless, bum."

WOMAN: (Hand held up to mouth) "How can you talk about him like that if he is God?"

MAN: "Why not? What will he do? Highlight this page and hit the delete key? I wish that he would. Didn't I just ask him to do this?"

WOMAN: (Speaking slowly, hesitantly, voice shaking.) "But I thought you were just angry. I thought that you were speaking carelessly."

MAN: "No. I meant it then, I mean it now."

WOMAN: (Almost crying) "But why? Why do you want us destroyed?"

MAN: (Walking up to WOMAN and putting his hands on her shoulders.) "Look, you are a beautiful woman, and I don't want to scare you, but you have to realize that you are *not*."

WOMAN: (Starting to cry) "What? What do you mean? Must you speak in riddles?"

MAN: (Softer now, stepping closer, looking WOMAN in the eye.) "You are not. I am not. This room, this universe is not. Yes we exist now, in this time in this place, but we are *not*, not real, not alive. We are the fabrications of an inebriated derelict of a man that can't do anything successfully in his own life so he sits in front of a computer making up the lives of others. He fancies himself to be an 'author'."

WOMAN: (Angrily stepping back from the MAN) "Your wrong!"

MAN: (Still speaking softly, stepping forward and embracing WOMAN) "I wish for your sake that I was—but I am not wrong."

WOMAN: (Breaking MAN's grip) "How do you know all of this? What makes you so damn clever?"

MAN: (Hanging his head, taking deep breath, then looking up, speaking resolutely) "Because I have been here before. Because I am him, I am the Creator."

WOMAN: (Shouting) "Sacrilege! (Backing away from MAN.) Get away from me! I have to leave here before you destroy us both." (WOMAN runs toward stage front, hits an invisible "wall"—noise heard off-stage sounds like a fist striking an empty 5-gallon water bottle—and falls down in a heap. Stunned she lays there while softly sobbing.)

MAN: (Walks over to WOMAN and stands over her. Speaking gently.) "You poor little fool. Must you torture yourself so? (Looking up at the ceiling and shouting, shaking his fist) Must you torture her, too? Aren't you satisfied with tormenting me?"

WOMAN: (Looks up, pathetically, still softly sobbing.) "Where *are* we? What is this place?"

MAN: (Taking a step towards the invisible "wall" and strikes it twice—same noise heard off stage again) "This is where he sees the words that make up you and me. (Pointing towards the audience while looking at WOMAN, she follows where his hand is pointing.) Out there, somewhere is the Creator."

MAN: (Helping WOMAN up.) "Now come away from here."

(WOMAN goes willingly to the center of the stage, looking back in fear at the "wall". At center stage, MAN puts his arms around her waist.)

MAN: For whatever it is worth, you are the most stunning character that he has ever teamed me with—and I have had some exquisite partners."

WOMAN: (Softly, putting her arms around MAN's waist.) I don't understand. You are so nice and gentle yet you say you are the Creator, the one who keeps us captive. How can you be both?"

MAN: "Yes I said I was him, and this is true, but not entirely. While I do look like him . . . ."

WOMAN: (Breaking away, excitedly) Yes! You were made in his image. That is how I believe."

MAN: (Looking like he is going to get angry—then deciding against it. Speaking slowly as if he were choosing his words) "Yes, I know you believe that way, I know why too, but don't interrupt again. Let me explain."

WOMAN: (Somewhat put off, taking a step back) "Okay, say what you will."

MAN: "What I said is that I look like him, but I am not him. I am often what he wants to be, but not always. Sometimes he likes how he makes me and he will print me out to keep in his drawer. Or he will send my adventures and me to publishers to see if they will print my anecdotes. So far, none have done so."

WOMAN: "But . . . ."

MAN: (Hand going up, pointing) "You promised you wouldn't interrupt!"

WOMAN: (Sarcastically, hands on hips) "Sorry!"

MAN: (Takes a deep breath.) "No, I'm sorry. I know that this must be confusing to you, but let me finish."

(WOMAN silently gestures acceptance with her hands.)

MAN: "We, you and I (points at WOMAN then back to himself), are but works of fiction. We don't exist in the so-called 'real world' of the Creator. We are *not*! And we may vanish at any time, erased in a fit of anxiety or drunken stupor. I can never tell when this might happen, but I know all this is true because I have died many deaths at his hands."

WOMAN: (Shortly, hands on hips.) "Now you make no sense!" (WOMAN puts up her hand to stop MAN who was about to reply.) Let me speak! How can you have died and yet still exist? Are you immortal? Have you risen from the grave like the God's son?"

MAN: (Hands at temples, grimacing) "No, no, no, no! You don't understand! I know all this because I have been here before, (Drops hand to chest level) I am what you might call a 'recurring character'; sometimes I am a fighting man, sometimes an athlete, and sometimes even a lover. (Drops hand in resignation, slowly shaking his head.) Whenever the Creator gets to feeling morose or angry at himself he calls me up and makes me do all the things that he wishes he could do."

WOMAN: "But why are you here, now. Why am I here?"

MAN: (Takes a deep breath.) "I am not sure of what we are a part of now. That is why I asked if God was dead. I feel (hesitantly) . . . incomplete. This universe we are in seems incomplete. I was wondering if the Creator may have died leaving us in the hands of who ever may next view the words that make up our pathetic existence. Yet then if this is true, how do I now speak? If he has died or abandoned us, how do I now question his very existence?"

WOMAN: "You have free will. You can do as you wish."

MAN: "But I, but we, cannot. Don't you see this? We are but his creations. We do as he says, we feel as he feels, we are a part of him that has made us."

WOMAN: "So we have no free will?"

MAN: "Of course not. You, as a religious character, should know this. God, whoever, whatever, that god is, plans your every step, every thought. We are puppets on a string."

WOMAN: (Excited again) "You are wrong, you must be wrong."

MAN: "I wish I were wrong, but I am not. I am not! I am nothing but a puppet. See the puppet walk! (Walks stage left, walks stage right, walks back to WOMAN imitating the walk of a marionette). See the puppet dance! (Dances in circle around WOMAN, imitating the dance of a marionette). See the puppet laugh! (Puts hands on stomach, while mouthing—no sound—laughter) See the puppet cry! (Bends forward, head down, limp from the waist, arms hanging freely for about 5 seconds) See the puppet die!" (Falls in a limp heap at WOMAN's feet).

WOMAN:(Waving her arms over MAN, palms down, as if they were knives cutting at the imagined strings of a marionette) "Get up, get up! You are wrong. I can prove it! I can prove it!"

MAN:(Standing, brushing himself off, bemused) "Now what idea is floating around in that pretty little head of yours?"

WOMAN: (Still excited, pointing at MAN) "Just that! My 'pretty little head', as you call it, is what makes your ideas so wrong. You say you are made in his image, yet how do you explain me. I am a woman, (Again WOMAN holds up her hand to stop MAN from interrupting), and I am, of this I am positive. I am also positive that you are a man. So how does the creator make us in his image when we are so different? How do you explain this?"

(MAN approaches WOMAN again and attempts to put his arms around her, but she steps back, to avoid his grasp.)

MAN: (Imploringly) "Don't turn away from me, please! As little as this universe has, at least it has you and I and we can be together. At least that way we will not be so lonely, so left out."

(WOMAN takes a step closer to MAN)

MAN: "Truthfully, I have been thinking about just that as you have."

WOMAN: "See! I was right!"

MAN: (Calmly, emphatically, palm up gesturing with his hand.) No you were not right. Remember—I have been here before, I have seen other men and women that the Creator has made for me to interact with, yet you *are* different from anyone else he has contrived for me."

WOMAN: (Standing sullenly, not saying a word, but allowing MAN to put his arms around her. She looks at MAN and puts her arms around his waist, speaking plaintively she lays her head on his shoulder, looking at the audience.) "Then tell me who you *think* I am."

MAN: "I will try. (Hesitates, looking up just over WOMAN's head, then looking directly into her eyes.) Sometimes, when the Creator drinks to excess, like he must have done tonight, he begins to explore his own being. When he is drunk he is in the one state of mind where he can be honest with himself, the one state where he can see what he is without being totally repulsed. I think that tonight he is reflecting his past. You represent the ideas he was brought up to believe about God and his own mortality while I, on the other hand, represent his current self doubts about God and religion. Even as I speak these words he is examining these divergent beliefs."

WOMAN: "But I am also a woman."

MAN: (Kisses WOMAN, holds it for a few seconds) "Yes, my dear, of that there is no doubt. In this way you represent something the Creator read. It was written by one of the people in his universe. Freud, I think, or maybe it was Heinlein, I am not sure. (Left hand goes to left temple, begins to speak breathlessly). Sorry, something is happening that is making it hard to think. (Takes a deep breath) Anyway, one of these people wrote about the bi-polarity of the sexes and how this phenomenon keeps his world moving. How the clash of human sex drive and the repression of it by those who are most tempted by it, represent a negative energy that powers everything in his universe. Our creator now thinks that without this conflict the world would stop turning so he includes a sexy lover in every story. (Hand goes back around WOMAN's waist, speaking haltingly) Even in our dress, me being all in black, you being all in white, he is exhibiting the differences between us. (MAN's hand goes back to his temple, grimacing) And yet, and yet, I may be all wrong about this. You may have been right after all. I can never know."

WOMAN: (Looking up at the ceiling.) "Stop it! What are you doing to him? Leave him alone!"

MAN: (Still speaking haltingly, hand down, still grimacing) "Don't beg or bow down to him, please. It's not really me that he is tormenting, it is himself for I am he; I am his other half, the reasoning half, the one that sees the world as it really is and not as it is on his television. He hates me. He hates his world. He wants it to be as he sees it but he feels powerless to do anything to make it so. That is why he sits at his computer making up the fantasy worlds that you and I populate."

WOMAN: (Looks at MAN) "I don't care!" (Looks back up at the ceiling) "Stop it! Leave us alone, leave us alone!"

MAN: (Also looking up at the ceiling) "Yes, leave us alone. We are happy now, we are together; is that not what you wanted? (Pulling the WOMAN closer to him) Leave us alone!"

MAN & WOMAN: (In chorus, looking up at the ceiling) "LEAVE US ALONE!"

(With a loud clicking sound, all the stage lights go out! Instant darkness. Neither MAN nor WOMAN can be seen. Wait for crowd reaction to subside—or ten seconds—what ever is longest! Then close curtains. A single spotlight illuminates center stage)

MAN: (Steps through the curtains at center stage.) I'm sorry folks, there really was suppose to be more to this. Unfortunately, God passed out before he could finish it."

(From behind the curtain, WOMAN's voice calls out in a sexy, hot voice) "Honey, are you coming to bed? I'm wearing the black lace negligee you like so much!"

(MAN, with a big smile on is face, winks, half salutes the audience, turns around and walks back into the folds of the curtain as the spotlight fades to black.)

THE END